INSIDE OUT

Other books by
ANN M. MARTIN

Yours Turly, Shirley

Ten Kids, No Pets

Slam Book

Just a Summer Romance

Missing Since Monday

With You and Without You

Me and Katie (the Pest)

Stage Fright

Bummer Summer

BABY-SITTERS LITTLE SISTER series

THE BABY-SITTERS CLUB series

ANN M. MARTIN

INSIDE OUT

AN
APPLE
PAPERBACK

SCHOLASTIC INC.
New York Toronto London Auckland Sydney

This book is for
FRANKIE, ELLIE, RON, BOBBY,
JIMMY, NICOLE, SCOTT, ARTHUR,
DREW, JILL, ARI, MARK, SANDY
SUSIE, MICHAEL, MITCHELL, *and*
all the other children who
tried as hard as they could.

The author would like to thank Dr. Barbara Kezur, PhD,
for her sensitive evaluation of the manuscript.

ISBN 0-590-43621-X

12 11 10 9 8 7 6 5   3 4 5/9

Printed in the U.S.A.   40

Contents

1. James

Saturday night I got about three hours of sleep. My mother says this is not natural for an eleven-year-old boy. I'd have to agree with her there. But it wasn't my fault. It was because of James. I could only have gotten more sleep if I'd slept somewhere else—somewhere where there is no boy who screams all night.

The screamer is my brother. James is four. We don't have a nickname for him. You have to know a person pretty well before you can give him a nickname. Like, if we knew him better we could decide if he was a Jamie or a Jim or a Jimmy. But we hardly know James at all. He has a lot of problems.

I have several nicknames myself. My real name is Jonathan Eckhardt Peterson. Most people call me Jon. My parents and sister call me Jonno, which is what I called myself when I was little. And my friends Pete and Termite call me Mac. This is because of my feet. They're sort of large. Actually they're huge. And when Pete and Termite and I were in third grade, a substitute showed us a really dumb movie about a kid named Mac. Mac happened to have huge feet, like mine. So Pete and Termite started calling me Mac. They thought it was hysterical, but the humor in it faded pretty quickly for me. Unfortunately, the name stuck. (How Termite, whose parents call him Charles, got his nickname is another story.)

The morning after the no-sleep night was a Saturday, and I felt rotten. My head ached and my eyes burned. Dad said now I knew what a hangover felt like. I wondered why anyone would want to know that. I was tempted to get back in bed since James was finally quiet, but it was better not to. I'd never get to sleep that night if I slept during the day.

So I sat out on my front porch. That's what I do when I'm bored or tired. I figured Pete or Termite would show up pretty soon. It was only March, but we'd had a few days of warm weather, and it was sunny and about sixty-five degrees. Sure enough, the weather and the sight of me on the porch brought Pete and Termite out in twenty minutes.

Pete came first. He's my oldest friend. We have the same birthday. Our mothers shared a room in the hospital when we were born, and our families have been friends ever since.

"Hi, Mac," Pete said. He sat down beside me on our stoop. He had his new baseball and glove with him.

"Hi," I said.

"Wanna toss a few?"

"Nah."

Pete looked at me. I knew my eyes were bloodshot.

"James again?" he asked. He understands about James.

"Yeah," I said. "From ten-thirty till almost five. Nonstop."

"Whew. That must be some kind of record."

I grinned. "Probably."

Pete likes records and projects and keeping track of things. He's serious about his projects. Once he turned his bookshelves into a real, honest-to-goodness lending library. The books were all categorized and arranged in some kind of order, and they had borrowing cards in flaps on the back, and Pete had figured out this lending system. The library lasted two weeks, and then Pete wanted to set up a wax museum in the garage, but his parents said no. I could see their point, but I like all Pete's projects. Some of them are really wild. You never know what to expect.

We sat in the sun. I was so tired I had to lean up against a post. Pete tossed the ball back and forth from one hand to the other. *Slap, slap. Slap, slap. Slap, slap.* It was putting me to sleep.

Luckily, Termite arrived.

"Hey, everyone," he said with a grin. Termite is just about always happy. He looks a little like a clown with his shock of bright red hair and freckles all across his nose and cheeks.

"Hey, Termite," Pete and I said, grinning back.

In some ways, Termite's different from Pete and me. He usually prefers to keep his ideas to himself and let other people do the thinking. He's kind of like the caboose on a train. But the three of us, he and Pete and I, always hang around together.

Pete filled Termite in on James and last night. Termite nodded. He knows about James, but he doesn't really understand. Not the way Pete does. He may be a little afraid of James, although he's never said so. But sometimes when James is nearby, Termite will disappear.

What with the warmth of the day and me being so tired and all, the three of us just sat around. My parents hate it when we do this, even though we don't do it often, because of Pete and his ideas. Dad says sitting around is unproductive.

After a while, Lizzie came out. She was wearing these Ronald McDonald sunglasses and this old red baseball cap. Lizzie's hair tends to frizz out all over the place, so she hides it under the cap whenever possible. Lizzie is my sister. She's eight going on nine. Her real name is Elizabeth, but nobody, including our grandmother, calls her that. It's because Lizzie is so definitely a Lizzie, and not an Elizabeth. I think an Elizabeth would be a prim, tidy person, and that's just not Lizzie.

Lizzie slumped down next to me. She was as tired as I was.

"Daddy went to the office this morning," she said miserably.

"I know," I answered.

I saw Pete and Termite exchange looks. They know about this, too. We have no secrets.

When things get rough with James, Dad sometimes can't handle it, so he escapes for a while, usually to the office. He's a lawyer. It's not fair that he skips out and leaves us—well, Mom mostly—to handle James, but maybe he can't help himself.

"Come on, you guys," said Pete brightly, "we have to think of something to *do*."

"Yes," I said. "Something quiet."

"Whatever."

We all thought.

"Hey!" Pete cried almost at once. (He's always the first one to get an idea.) "We could have a lemonade stand. Except not just a plain old lemonade stand. It would be more of a snack bar. We could sell lemonade and ice tea and punch. And make Popsicles by freezing Kool-Aid in paper cups with sticks in them. And sell popcorn and frozen bananas, too."

"Yeah!" said Termite.

"Nah," said Lizzie.

"Nah," said I.

We went back to thinking.

"Hey!" cried Pete again. "I know! I've got some caps—"

"I thought your mother confiscated them," I interrupted.

"Only the ones she could find," said Pete. "So we take the caps and get a hammer and find out how high dogs jump when they're scared by exploding caps."

"Yeah!" said Termite.

"Nah," said Lizzie.

"Nah," said I.

Pete leaned back, whistling and thinking. Luckily, he doesn't get upset if you don't like his ideas. Besides, today he knew it was because Lizzie and I were tired.

Finally someone else had an idea. "Well," said Termite. (I knew he was going to suggest making goof calls. I just knew it.) "We could make goof calls," he said.

"Nah," said Pete.

"Nah," said Lizzie.

"Nah," said I.

Termite looked a little hurt.

"I'm sorry," I said. "But you always want to make goof calls, and we've done it so often the fun's running out. Not that we don't enjoy it. But we just made a bunch on Thursday."

Making goof calls was how Termite got his nickname. See, one day he got this terrific idea while we were huddled around the phone in his kitchen. (We make our goof calls from Termite's house because no one's ever there. Termite has two half sisters who are away at college, and both his parents work. Pete's an only child, but his mother works at home, so she's there practically all the time, and she's on the phone a lot, too.)

Termite's terrific idea was to pretend he was a termite exterminator. The idea was a little risky, but it worked often enough to be fun. We'd go through the phone book and pick out a number that sounded like a home phone number. Then Termite would make the call. When someone answered, he'd say, "Hello, this is the Armstrong Exterminating Company. Your husband" (or wife, depending) "just called me from work and told me about the termite problem you're having."

Usually the person wouldn't believe him, but Termite could be pretty convincing.

Then he'd try to set up an appointment to come over with his equipment. That first day he made two actual appointments (both of which he politely canceled later). From then on, as far as Pete and I were concerned, his name was no longer Charles Anthony Armstrong III. It was Termite.

After the goof call suggestion, we were running out of ideas. At last Pete said, "Let's just go shoot a few baskets. Nothing strenuous."

I groaned. "O.K."

"O.K.," said Lizzie.

"Aw, Lizzie," I said.

Now, don't get me wrong. I like Lizzie a lot. So do Pete and Termite. And I don't mind if she wants to hang around with us, but she's not a hot basketball player.

"Please, Jonno," she begged.

It kills me when she does that.

"You need someone to even up your teams," she went on.

"They're already even," Termite joked. "Mac's so tired he doesn't count."

We headed for our driveway where Dad had installed a hoop at the end of the turn-around.

Lizzie ran alongside us, still wanting to play. "Pretty puh-*lease,* with sugar on top."

Pete rolled his eyes.

Before we could even find the basketball, Dad drove up. He looked calm, which was a good sign.

We rushed up to the car and waited for him to get out. "Hi, Daddy," squealed Lizzie.

"Hi, sweetheart," he said, giving her a kiss. "Great glasses."
She touched the Ronalds on the frames and giggled.

"Hi, Dad," I said.

"Hi, son. Hi, Pete, Charles. What are you up to today?"

"Four feet, ten inches," said Termite.

It was an old, old joke between them. We laughed anyway.

Then we heard a terrible screech. We all turned around.
James came bolting out of the garage. He was only half dressed
(the top half). and he was galloping around and wringing his
hands. "Weee-oooh, weee-oooh, weee-oooh," he wailed.

He was really upset, but he wasn't crying tears. He hardly
ever does; just wails and groans.

He headed right for us like he couldn't see us, but at the
last minute he made a detour.

"For crying out—" my father started to say crossly.

Mom appeared at the garage door holding James's pants.
"James!" she shouted.

Everything was happening so fast.

"Weee-oooh," cried James frantically.

He doesn't speak.

Pete and I made a grab for him, catching him by the arms.
We carried him back to Mom, who was standing with Dad
now. She picked him up and tried to calm him down as they
went into the house.

When Pete and I turned around, Lizzie was on the monkey
swing under the elm tree where she goes when she's upset.
Termite was disappearing through his front door.

Darn old James. Why does he have to ruin everything?

2. A School for James

If anyone had seen my family at dinner that night, they'd have thought we were pretty weird. First of all, we were so tired we were practically falling off our chairs. Second, Lizzie was wearing her baseball cap at the table. Mom and Dad don't make her take it off because they know how she feels about her hair. Third, Mom and Dad and Lizzie and I were eating fried chicken, broccoli, and rice, while James was slowly working his way through a cup of dry Cheerios and half a plain bagel.

This is another thing about James. Eating. The only foods he'll eat without any fuss are Cheerios, bagels, Hawaiian Punch, and milk. At most meals Mom and Dad take turns forcing him to eat normal food. They have to feed him the way you'd feed a baby. Sometimes Lizzie or I give them a break and take over. Then, after you've been feeding him meat and vegetables and stuff for about fifteen minutes, he usually barfs them up. I can't tell you the number of meals that have ended with James puking all over the place. Mom and Dad think it's worth it for the few times he keeps the healthy stuff down. Personally, I think it's revolting.

Also James hardly ever sits still. The doctor's word for this is "hyperactive." James is forever squirming, wiggling, and running around. Meals are especially bad, and so James still eats in a highchair. We have to strap him in. It's the only way to keep him in one spot.

This evening, though, no one was about to force-feed James anything. We just let him go to town on his Cheerios. It was a much pleasanter meal.

"Well, kids," said Dad, "how was everybody's day?" (He'd gone back to the office right after he'd helped Mom get James's pants on.)

"Fine, Daddy," said Lizzie tiredly. "Me and Wendell caught minnows in Harry's Brook."

Lizzie has almost no girlfriends, and no friends her age. Either she hangs around with Pete and Termite and me, or she bugs Wendell to do stuff with her. Wendell is at least fifteen.

"What about you, Jonno?" Dad asked.

"Well, Pete and Termite wanted me to look for golf tees for Mr. Armstrong at the shopping center this afternoon, but I didn't feel like it. I read this book I have to do a report on instead."

Right then James coughed, and we all lunged at him with napkins, positive he was going to throw up, even though he was eating Cheerios. Luckily, it was just a regular cough. James looked up, startled to see us coming at him. Then his eyes glazed over, and he reached for the bagel, as if we weren't even there.

My mother sighed.

"Any word?" asked my father. "I know it's Saturday . . . but you never know."

"No. Maybe next week," said Mom.

They were talking about James's school. This really great

thing had happened. After a couple of years of dragging James around from doctor to doctor and specialist to specialist, they'd found a program, right in the next town, that James could join as soon as there was an opening. The school is only for kids like James. James is autistic.

It took us forever to find that out. See, way back when James was two, this big change came over him. Until then he'd been a pretty normal baby, except that he didn't like to be held or picked up. But he could talk and feed himself, and he was almost toilet-trained, and he liked to play with Lizzie and me. Then (and it happened awfully quickly) he started talking less and less until finally he wasn't talking at all, just making funny sounds like *weee-oooh*. We didn't know *what* had happened. The eating and sleeping problems started, and he stopped wanting to run around after Lizzie and me. Instead he started sitting alone for hours, rocking himself back and forth or waving his hands in front of his eyes or spinning pennies on the bathroom floor. If you touched him or interrupted him, he'd scream.

Now, more than two years later, he's still like that, except when he gets hold of my old Lincoln Logs, or Lizzie's Legos or Tinkertoys. Then he builds these huge, amazing structures. They're really complicated. I don't know how they stand up half the time, but they do. Mom and Dad look at the structures and say James can't be retarded. The buildings are so complex even Pete couldn't make them.

Another reason Mom says James can't be retarded is that he doesn't *look* retarded. When he's not doing something weird, he has this bright, serious look on his face, as if inside his head he's thinking complicated thoughts, as complicated as his buildings. I like to imagine that James doesn't want to have anything to do with us because he's this fantastic genius, and our world is too dull for him, compared with the high-level stuff he's working on in his head. Sometimes I'll come upon him when he's staring—not spinning or waving or wailing—just staring, and I'll watch him sitting with his blond hair falling in his big brown eyes, and I'll think, James, I bet you're smarter than all of us. Then I'll remember about him spinning pennies and only eating Cheerios, and I'll think, No, James, you're just a mystery to me.

Anyway, before we found out James was autistic, Mom and Dad spent months taking him from one doctor to another, trying to find someone who could help him, someone who could tell us what was wrong. Sometimes they'd be gone for a day or two, sometimes for a week or two. Lizzie and I didn't go with them. We'd stay at home, and Granny and Grandpoppy would come take care of us. That was sort of fun, but one time Lizzie got appendicitis while Mom and Dad and James were in Denver, and by the time Mom could fly back here to Massachusetts, the operation was over. Lizzie never forgave her. Or James. I could understand how she felt.

At first, none of the doctors could tell us what was wrong with James. One doctor said he was deaf and we should get a hearing aid for him, but that didn't make sense. Even though he acted like he couldn't hear us talking to him, he could hear the quietest sounds, like a paper rustling in another room. One doctor said he was hopelessly retarded and we should stick him in an institution. But we knew about his fantastic Tinker-toy creations. Another one said (get this) that James was just spoiled and the sooner we stopped treating him like a baby, the faster he'd grow out of his problems. That was stupid. Sandy Macey down the street was as spoiled as rotten eggs, but at least she could talk.

Then, a few months before James's fourth birthday, we

found this doctor in New York who said James seemed autistic, but he was too little for any testing. He suggested Mom and Dad take James home, wait six months, and bring him back for tests. He said our whole family could use a break from doctors. Thank you very, very much, Dr. Lewis, I thought, when Dad told me this.

The next six months were better. With the pressure of the doctors' visits off, James seemed a little more relaxed. You could touch him and he wouldn't scream. He'd let you hold his hand sometimes. But otherwise he was just the same. It was great to have Mom and Dad home, though.

James went back to the doctor in six months and was tested. The doctor said James was autistic, which was the first diagnosis that made sense to my parents. See, autism isn't a disease where your body gets sick and you can say you have a fever and a sore throat or a cough and a runny nose. Instead "autism" describes the way a person behaves. Most autistic kids, like James, act as if other people don't exist. They seem to be lost in their own world. They don't like to be touched, they don't talk, they don't go near people. Usually they get along with *things* better than people, like James spinning his pennies and staring at lights and building with Tinkertoys, and they can do the same things over and over and over again for hours.

Anyway, the doctor helped us find the school over in Weston. Now we were just waiting for them to have room for James. It could be any day, Mom said. We were hoping it would be soon because we couldn't take much more.

"Speaking of school," Dad said, and we all looked at him, wondering if he knew something we didn't, "there's something I've been meaning to say to you kids." Dad nodded at me and Lizzie.

"Us?" asked Lizzie.

I knew she was wondering the same thing I was. What did James's school have to do with us?

"Yes," said Dad. "As you know, having a child like James is expensive," he began.

Lizzie and I knew this. Some of those trips to doctors cost as much as a couple of thousand dollars. Insurance paid for some of it, but not everything. We couldn't take family vacations anymore, and we'd had to sell our cottage at Bayhead Beach.

"When James starts school, we'll have tuition to pay."

Lizzie and I must have looked a little blank, because Dad went on, "The Weston Child Development Institute is a private school. That means we have to pay to send James there. You two go to public school, which is free, but a private school is different."

"Oh," I said.

"What I'm getting at," said Dad as he finished the last of his chicken and pushed his plate away, "is that we're still paying off doctors' bills, and now we'll have tuition payments as well. When James starts school, your mother will have more time for her work" (she's a freelance copywriter), "but money's still going to be tight around here for a while. You'll continue to get your allowances, but if you want extras, you'll probably have to buy them yourselves, so you might want to think about earning some spending money."

"I understand," said Lizzie. She can be so serious.

"Me, too," I said. I wasn't thrilled, but I understood.

Mom and Dad smiled. They used to apologize to us about James, but not anymore. It doesn't do any good, and besides it's kind of mean to James.

Then Lizzie, even though she resents James, managed to

come through. "It will even be fun," she said. "Think of all
the things we can do, Jonno. I like earning money."

"Sure, Lizzie," I said, but without quite as much conviction.
I was thinking of the Build-Your-Own Starcruiser kit I wanted
so badly. It was real expensive—$62.99 at Kaler's Hardware
Store downtown. Every now and then Mr. Kaler would have
a sale, but even so, that Starcruiser would cost a lot of money.
I'd hoped Mom and Dad might pay for half of it if I paid for
the other half. They did that sometimes for Lizzie and me.
But now I'd just have to earn it all myself. No way could I
convince anybody that Starcruiser was a necessity. And my
birthday was months away. I tried to look on it as a challenge.
I knew just how to start, too. I'd call Pete.

Dad volunteered to clean up dinner since he'd been off the
hook with James all day, so as soon as I was excused I dashed
into the den and dialed Pete's number.

"Hmmm," said Pete slowly, after I explained the situation.
I could tell he was excited that I needed one of his ideas.
"Remember that electric belt-buckler I almost invented last
year? Maybe we could perfect it and patent it. Then we could
round up Termite and Lizzie and mass-produce them and sell
them. The belt-bucklers, I mean. Not Termite and Lizzie."
Pete is always very precise.

I thought a minute. "Got anything less complicated? I don't
want to take too long to earn the money."

"Hmmm," said Pete again.

I tapped my fingers and waited.

"Maybe we could pool all our money and invest it in the
stock market."

"*Pete*. You have to have thousands of dollars to do that."

"Oh. Well. Hang on a minute."

I hung.

"Hey!" he cried.

I perked up a little. That sounded like a pretty promising "hey."

"What we need to do is start a business."

"Yeah?" I said excitedly.

"And for it to be profitable, we have to do something people won't have to pay *too* much for. That way they'll be more willing to do business with us."

"Yeah?" I cried. This was getting good.

"And it has to be something that's not too taxing on us. That way it's worth our while."

"Yeah! What do you have in mind? What kind of business?"

"I don't know."

"Oh."

"But I'll come up with something. I'd like to earn some money, too. I've got a long way to go on my mother's birthday present."

Pete and I hung up. He wanted me to come over and watch a horror movie on TV, but I was too tired. I wanted to go right to bed.

I headed for the stairs, but when I got to the living room I came across James and one of his structures. It was made from Tinkertoys. He does his best work with Tinkertoys.

"Hey, James," I said. I always talk to him, even though he won't answer. For all I know, maybe he tunes out human voices. But just in case, I talk to him pretty much. "That's neat, James," I went on. "This is one of your biggest ones. I wish you could tell me what it is. Is it a space station? Or an office building?"

James was standing on tiptoe, concentrating intently on attaching some pieces to the top.

I watched him working. He was straining so hard his arms

were shaking. I could hear him humming under his breath. He
was humming a Bach piece he had heard this morning. James
has an incredible memory for music. Any song he hears, even
just once, he remembers completely. Just the tune, of course,
not the words. And it doesn't matter whether it's Stravinsky
or REO Speedwagon.

"Want some help, James?" I asked, thinking no four-year-
old should work so hard.

He didn't pay any attention. So far he hadn't even looked
at me.

I saw what he was trying to do—to get one of the little
round pieces on one of the sticks at the very top of the building,
but he wasn't quite tall enough to reach.

"Here," I said. I started to take the piece from his hand.

Still without looking at me, he snatched his hand away and
sort of danced around to the other side of the building. "Weee-
oooh," he said anxiously. It sounded like a warning.

"Well, good night, James," I said finally, and went quietly
up the stairs. But when I got to my room, I slammed the door.

I hope James heard it, and I hope he jumped. After all, I
was only trying to help him.

3. Edweird

Monday morning.

Pete and Termite and I were sitting in our classroom talking. Mr. Westoff, our teacher, lets us do that when we're not officially in class. Right then we had twelve minutes until the first bell rang.

I was sitting on my desk, Pete was sitting on his desk, and Termite was sitting on Margaret Sesselbaum's desk. Termite's not in our class, but he comes in before the bell to talk sometimes.

It was pretty brave of him to sit on Margaret's desk. Margaret wouldn't like to know that someone as lowly as Termite Armstrong had been sitting on her desk, smelling it up. Even if she didn't come in early enough to see him, she'd hear about it from Louise Werner or Janie Cunningham or Elise Markey. Probably Elise. Elise is the leader of that particular group. They are the in-girls in my classroom. The four of them are pretty and smart, act like they're better than everyone, and do things to impress the in-boys.

Needless to say, Pete and I are not in-boys. The in-boys of the class are David Lowe, Hank Read, Chris Giancossi, and

17

Alan Steinwick. There is no leader, no Elise, among them. But it doesn't matter. They are just like the in-girls, basically. They are good-looking, smart, and think they're great.

Pete and I aren't exactly shunned by the in-kids, but we hang around on the edge of things. We don't fit in. To them, we're uncool. We're the wrong way around, or upside down, or inside out. Maybe inside out describes us best. We're no good at hiding what's wrong with us. It all shows. The in-kids must have some secret for covering up their feelings when they're dumb or gawky or insecure. The rest of us let everything hang out. Unfortunately.

Termite was talking about how his half sisters would be home from college for spring vacation soon, and Elise and her crew were drifting in. They huddled in a corner, whispering, and didn't even notice Termite on Margaret's desk. Lucky for him.

Then David, Alan, Hank, and Chris sauntered in. Their saunters looked terribly nonchalant. Too nonchalant, if you know what I mean. They seated themselves very, very casually on some desks not too far from the huddle going on in the corner. I noticed that the voice level in the huddle rose just enough so the boys could hear.

There are two girls in the class who are kind of like me and Pete—not in with Elise, but not as far gone as some others. They are Stephanie Kautzmann and Claudia Smith. I happen to like Steph and Claud a lot. For one thing, they don't spend a lot of time poking at their faces in mirrors or whispering about Dave and Hank and Chris and Alan. For another, they're nice to everybody, including the stuck-up in-kids *and* Termite and me and Pete. Sometimes me and Pete and Steph and Claud hang out together. We always try to be a group when group project time rolls around.

The best thing about Steph and Claud is that they don't care much what Elise and everyone thinks of them. I wish I could say the same for myself. I do care. I'm not sure why. I waver between wanting to be one of the in-boys and liking being just myself, goofing around with Pete and Termite.

I was thinking about the little groups that always form in a classroom, when the bell rang. Termite shot off Margaret's desk and charged out the door without saying good-bye. He only had two minutes to get all the way down the hall and around the corner to his classroom before the final bell would ring. He always makes it.

Mr. Westoff usually comes in right after the first bell. Sure enough, in a few seconds the door opened, and in he walked. But he wasn't alone. He held the door open for a very large boy. Well, all right, he was fat. He had his pants hitched up with a belt I could have wrapped three or four times around my waist.

I looked closer. The bottoms of his pants were way above his ankles. A lot of sock showed. And he was wearing a pair of those fancy brown leather shoes with holes punched all over the tops. All the guys wear running shoes. Right away I knew he'd be in for a lot of teasing. I checked over my right shoulder and saw Alan Steinwick laughing uncontrollably into his math book, and David Lowe laughing uncontrollably into his desk, and Chris Giancossi laughing uncontrollably into his lap as he bent over to tie his shoe, supposedly. Hank Read couldn't find anything to laugh uncontrollably into, so he was just turning red from holding it in.

I looked back at the boy. He was about fourteen. Much too old for our class. Just a visitor, thank goodness, so he wouldn't have to endure the laughter too long. I could sympathize. I know what it's like to be laughed at.

The last thing I expected was for Mr. Westoff to face the class, put his arm across the boy's shoulders, and say, "Everybody, this is Edward Jackson. He's going to join our class." Then he added rather pointedly, "I hope you'll make him feel welcome."

Oh, brother. He was a new kid, not a visitor!

Mr. Westoff started to guide Edward to an empty seat over by the door, but Edward continued facing us. "Hi," he said nervously. "I'm glad to meet you. My name is Edward Jackson."

The laughter was spreading. It had contaminated Margaret, Elise, and Janie. It was about to catch up with Louise.

I glanced over at Pete. He just looked surprised. Then I looked at Claud and Steph. Claud was staring intently at her hands. She looked almost sad. Steph was glaring at Elise. It wasn't doing any good.

"Come on, Ed," said Mr. Westoff brightly. "Here's your desk." He led Edward down an aisle.

Edward never stopped talking. "This is a nice school. Where's the water fountain, Mr. Westoff?"

He passed Alan's desk. "Do you like this school? Do you know where the gym is?"

The laughter wasn't silent anymore.

"Where—where's the pencil sharpener, Mr. Westoff? Where's the nurse's office, Mr. Westoff?"

Edward sat at his desk and turned around to Elise, who sat behind him. Unfortunately.

"Where's the—the cafeteria?" he said to her.

I guess it was the thought of Edward adding to his bulk that set everyone off even more. The room was filled with snickers and snorts. Even I was beginning to feel the urge. Not because of poor Edward; just because of all the other laughter. It was rising up in me. I pursed my lips and put my hand over my mouth, managing to laugh silently. I looked over at Pete and saw he was doing the same thing. I felt a little better.

Mr. Westoff was still trying to get Edward settled quietly, helping him put his things in his desk.

Suddenly a note landed in my lap. It didn't come from Pete's direction. I opened it quickly, keeping an eye on Mr. Westoff.

The note said:

> I wonder what planet he comes from?

It was signed *Chris*.

Chris Giancossi?

Sending poor, out-of-it Jonathan E. Peterson a note? Well, I *was* sitting closer to him than any of the in-boys were.

Quickly I scribbled back:

> Planet Fat?
> Planet of the Blimps?
> Planet of the Oven Stuffer Roasters?

I tossed the note to Chris. He read it, scrunched it up, and grinned at me.

I grinned back, feeling ridiculously happy.

Mr. Westoff had finally gotten Edward seated and quiet. As soon as he left him, Edward turned around to Elise, stuck out his hand, and said, "I'm pleased to meet you. My name is Edward Jackson. I'm thirteen-and-a-half-years old."

Elise blushed and busily sorted through her desk. She didn't even look at Edward.

Edward looked hurt and turned around, facing front. He was the most inside-out person I had ever seen.

I was torn between wanting to feel sorry for him and wanting to grin at Chris.

Mr. Westoff took attendance and collected our homework

papers, and we pledged allegiance to the flag.

After the pledge, a messenger appeared at the door.

Mr. Westoff waved her in and said, "O.K. Edward, find your math book, your speller, your reader, and some pencils. This is Sandy Castleman. She'll take you to the Resource Room."

Chris looked over at me and raised an eyebrow. The Resource Room. We all knew what that was. The place for the problem kids.

Everyone watched Edward get his stuff together. He put his math book on top of the pile. It was a *second-grade* book. I looked at Chris and knew he had seen, too.

Just as Sandy was about to lead Edward out the door, he turned around and said loudly, "Good-bye, Mr. Westoff. Good-bye, everybody. I'll be back for lunch."

Snicker, snicker.

Snort, snort.

Chris leaned over and whispered to me. "Hey, his name shouldn't be Edward. It should be Ed*weird.*"

"Yeah!" I said.

Right after Edward left, Mr. Westoff had a little talk with all of us.

Even so, by the end of the day, every kid in the class knew about Edward's new name.

4. "I'll Be Rich!"

"So," I said to Termite, as he and Pete and I walked home from school that afternoon, "Chris says, 'His name shouldn't be Edward. It should be Ed*weird*.'"

"He *is* a little strange," said Termite carefully. He'd seen Edweird on the playground after lunch.

"I'll say," I said.

"I'll say," Pete said.

"It's kind of too bad about him," Termite said.

"Yeah," I said.

"Yeah," Pete said.

Conversation lagged then. Funny how we were embarrassed to talk about Edweird.

We reached our houses and split up. Our parents have this rule. We have to get our homework done before we're allowed to fool around together on weekdays. Since we'd stayed after school for baseball practice today, there wasn't time left to do anything.

"See you tomorrow," we called to each other.

I ran up our front walk. "Hi, I'm home!" I yelled as soon as I walked through the door.

"*Shhhh,*" Lizzie hissed from the living room. She was dusting the tables. The house was very quiet.

"What's wrong?" I whispered. "Is someone sick?" I looked closer and saw that Lizzie was crying.

"Hey, Liz," I said. "What's the matter?" I dumped my stuff on the nearest chair and made her sit down on the couch with me.

She began crying so hard she couldn't talk, so I let her sniffle and sob for a while.

Finally I said again, "What's wrong, Lizzie?"

Sniffle. Sob. "It's James," she managed to say.

"Is he hurt?" I asked quickly.

Lizzie shook her head. The crying began to let up.

I straightened her baseball cap.

"I came home," she said, "and Mommy was lying on the couch with a washcloth over her eyes, and she'd been crying. I asked her what was wrong, and she said she'd taken James shopping again."

"Oh," I said.

Taking James shopping is never a good idea. He gets crazy in stores with all the people and all the stuff on the shelves and counters. He starts weee-ooohing after only five or ten minutes. Mom takes him in a stroller so he can't run around, but even so he makes a lot of noise, and people always stare. Sometimes he manages to struggle out of the stroller, and then it's all over. He starts the galloping bit, flinging his hands around. I always want to say to him, "James, it's really O.K. It's just a store. Nothing's going to hurt you." But it wouldn't make any difference.

Recently we've tried to arrange our days so James doesn't have to go shopping. Like, Mom will shop in the afternoons and leave him with me, or shop at night or on the weekends when Dad is home. But she can't do that all the time.

"What happened today?" I asked Lizzie.

"It was worse than usual," she said softly. "They were in the grocery store and Mommy was talking to someone, and before she knew it, James escaped from the stroller and ran away and knocked over a paper towel display. Then the manager yelled at Mommy in front of her friend and said children like James didn't belong in public."

We were both quiet for a while.

"Where are Mom and James now?" I asked after a bit.

"Mommy's taking a nap and...I hope you don't mind, Jonno—I put James in his room."

"That's O.K.," I said, and gave Lizzie a little smile.

I know it sounds mean, but we've fixed James's door so it locks from the outside. That way, when he gets out of control, or when we're too busy to watch him, we have a safe place to put him. There's nothing he can hurt himself on, and he certainly doesn't mind being alone. We don't put him there very often, but I could understand why Lizzie did it today.

"Any reason why you're dusting?" I asked her. "You hate housework."

"I know, but it was the only way I could get Mommy to take a nap. She said she was way, way behind on her job and the chores and the garden because darn old James has been so bad. So I told her I'd clean the living room and weed the front garden and finally she said O.K. But it's not fair, Jonno. It isn't. Why should we have to do all this just because of James? He never does anything around here. And he makes Mommy cry, and he makes Daddy upset."

Even though I agreed with Lizzie, all I said was, "I know. It isn't fair, but James is special. There's nothing we can do about that. So come on. I'll help you with the weeding. We should probably start dinner, too. Is there any spaghetti sauce?"

"Oh," Lizzie said flatly. "That's another thing. Daddy won't be home for dinner."

"He won't?"

"No." Lizzie sounded like she might cry again. "He called a little while ago, and when I said Mommy was taking a nap, he suddenly decided to work late. I guess he figured we were having trouble with James."

I nodded silently.

"Let's just have leftovers," Lizzie said. "Daddy won't be home and Mommy will be tired, and you know James and spaghetti."

I knew.

Disaster.

So Lizzie and I dusted and weeded and started the leftovers heating up, and then I remembered James. He was still locked in his room.

"I better go get James," I said as we finished setting the kitchen table.

Lizzie looked at me and didn't say anything.

I tiptoed upstairs, hoping I wouldn't wake Mom, and turned the lock on James's door.

James was kneeling on the floor in the exact middle of his room. The ceiling light was turned on. I wondered if he had done that himself. He was rocking back and forth, back and forth, gazing at the light and waving his right hand in front of his eyes.

"James," I said softly. I felt funny interrupting him.

He never paused. I don't think he even knew I was in his room.

"James," I said again, a little louder.

This time there was a slight hesitation in the rocking.

"Come on," I said to him. I reached out and took one of his hands very gently.

The rocking stopped.

"Let's go downstairs, James."

He stood up without a sound and let me lead him from his room. He is usually quite calm after he's been up there. I don't know if it's the room or the rocking.

Downstairs I sat James on the floor in the living room and gave him a pile of Legos. He didn't show any interest in them, but he didn't make any noise either.

When Mom came down to the living room a little after six, dinner was all ready, the chores were finished, Lizzie and I were doing our homework, and James was diddling a little red Lego between his fingers and humming a Beatles medley we'd just heard on the radio.

Mom looked bleary-eyed and tired and not really ready to face anything yet. She took the three of us in at a glance and smiled as she sank down on the couch. "How long has it been since I've told you guys how terrific you are? Look at this. You're doing your homework, dinner is cooking away—I can smell it—you've gotten James calmed down..." Her voice trailed off.

We almost always talk about James right in front of him, and lots of times we forget to include him as part of our family. Like right now, all three of us kids were in the living room, and Mom had said "you guys," but she was really only talking to Lizzie and me. It was sad.

"Thanks, Mom," I said, forcing a smile.

Lizzie ran over to her, and Mom gave her a big hug.

In about fifteen minutes we sat down at the kitchen table for dinner. Nobody said anything about Dad not being there. Lizzie had told Mom about the phone call, and that was the end of that.

We ate quietly, hardly talking. James was strapped into the highchair, picking at Cheerios and milk—separately. He won't eat Cheerios like regular cereal, and besides, he hates using a spoon. We had plenty of leftover broccoli and chicken, and some stew from last night, but after Mom's day, nobody was going to make James eat it. We were doing this more and more often recently. It wasn't very healthy for James.

"I guess the school didn't call today," I said foolishly, knowing Mom would have said something if they had.

Mom shook her head. "No. And I should face up to it— the director said they might not have an opening until September."

You'd have thought Mom would have been sad or angry, but she didn't look either way. Just like she was accepting it. I didn't know if that was good or bad.

After dinner Lizzie and I cleaned up while Mom tried to read a story to James. He usually doesn't pay any attention and hardly even sits still, but *sometimes* we think he might be looking at the pictures. So Mom keeps reading to him. Tonight, though, he ran away after three pages, and Mom was too tired to go after him, so that was the end of the story.

I finished my homework and took a pile of magazines up to my room. I closed the door. For some reason I didn't feel like talking to anybody.

I thumbed through the magazines, reading all the sports stories, and then I looked through the ads in back, just in case there was anything you could get free.

There wasn't much, but suddenly something caught my eye. It was an ad in a little box and it said:

MAKE MONEY FAST!

IT'S EASY, IT'S FUN!

You can earn as much as $10 a day—
in your spare time!

The ad went on a bit longer in very tiny letters. It turned out all you had to do was send fifty cents (for postage and handling) to the E-Z Seed Company, and they'd send you three hundred packages of vegetable and flower seeds. Then you were supposed to go from door to door selling the seeds. You got to keep twenty-five percent of whatever you earned. (You sent the other seventy-five percent back to the E-Z Seed Company.) I did some fast calculating and figured out I'd have to sell eighty packages of seeds to earn the ten dollars they were talking about.

Eighty packages a day. It seemed a little high, but who knows? Maybe it was really easy to sell seeds. After all, it was almost spring, and people were starting to plant their gardens.

I figured some more. If I could sell the eighty packages a day, I'd have enough money for the Starcruiser kit in just six and one-third days. That was a whole lot sooner than I'd expected. I'd thought it would take months to earn $62.99, even with Pete's help.

I scrounged around in my underwear drawer until I came up with two quarters. Then I filled out the order blank in the magazine and mailed everything off to the E-Z Seed Company.

At ten dollars a day, I'd be rich! Things were looking up.

5. Time-Savers, Inc.

The next Saturday I got up at eight o'clock after a good sleep. James hadn't made a peep at night since that awful time a week ago.

By eight-thirty I was seated at the kitchen table having breakfast by myself. On Saturday, everyone in my family eats on his own, since we kind of go our separate ways. Right now Lizzie was still asleep, Mom was working on an assignment that was due Monday, and Dad was gardening and keeping an eye on James, who wasn't doing much of anything.

I was digging into a big bowl of Rice Krispies when Pete appeared at the kitchen door. "Come on in," I called.

He came in and closed the door quickly behind him. It was a nice day out, but not as warm as it had been last Saturday.

"Mac, Mac," he cried. "Have I ever got an idea! Listen to this."

"What?" I asked excitedly. I knew it had to be the money-making scheme, and it had to be good. "Want some breakfast?"

"No, thanks," said Pete. "I just ate." But he helped himself to three pieces of toast anyway. He acts like this when he's got an especially fantastic idea.

"O.K.," he began. "I hope you got enough sleep last night

because we have a lot to do today."

"I got plenty," I said. "James has been really good lately."

"Great," said Pete. "O.K., here's the thing. We start an odd job service. You and Termite and I, and Lizzie if she wants. We'll do anything for anybody at a fixed rate of a dollar fifty an hour. We'll wash windows, walk dogs, baby-sit, mow lawns, paint, anything. What do you think?"

I was stuck back on "fixed rate." Pete's always coming up with these things I don't understand. How does he stay so far ahead of everyone?

"It sounds terrific," I said. "What's a fixed rate?"

"It means no matter what we're doing or who we're doing it for, we charge the same. A dollar fifty an hour."

"Oh," I said. "Hey, I think this is super. How do we let people know about us?" Between this and the E-Z Seed Company, I'd have more money than I'd know what do do with.

"I've got that all worked out. You know my old printing press? We'll print up fliers—ads—and stick them in mailboxes."

"Yeah! And we should have a name for us. We're sort of a company."

"Oh, right. Let's see."

We both thought for a minute.

"The Odd Job Service!" I suggested triumphantly.

"Too plain," said Pete. "We need something catchy."

"Time-Savers, Inc.," I said.

"Hey! I like that. That's really good. It's a name people will remember, and it says something they want to hear—we save them time."

"Right," I said, proud of myself for having come up with this particular idea.

"Let's go get Termite," said Pete.

I threw my dishes in the dishwasher and flew out the door

after Pete. "Going to the Armstrongs'," I yelled over my shoulder to Dad.

We collected Termite, who was very enthusiastic about the idea, and headed over to Pete's to use his printing press.

"The ad should tell all the things we'll do," said Pete as we settled ourselves in his room.

"And say we'll do anything else. Any odd job," added Termite.

"And it should have our names and phone numbers," I said.

"And the hours we can be reached."

"And the times we can work."

"And how much we charge."

At first we had trouble setting up all that information on Pete's press, but finally we got it together, and Pete cranked out one flier to see how we'd done.

This is what our ad looked like:

TIME-SAVERS, INC.

We save you time!
Lowest rates!

Do you hate gardening? Cleaning? Mowing your lawn?

Do you want your dog walked?

Do you need a baby-sitter?

Call us! We're here to help.

We'll do any odd job and we charge only $1.50 an hour.

Baby-sitting	Lawn mowing
Pet-sitting	Weed pulling
Cleaning	Painting
Gardening	Dog walking
Window washing	Car washing

And anything else you need done!

Call us now

Peter Wilson	921-5408
Jonathan Peterson	921-4932
Charles Armstrong	921-8611

Call after school or on the weekends.

We can work any afternoon and any Saturday or Sunday.

(We had decided our parents would ease up on the homework rule for something as important as running our business.)

We studied the ad carefully and decided it looked O.K. and that all the spelling was correct. Just to make sure, though, we took it downstairs and had Mrs. Wilson read it. When she finished, she smiled and said it looked fine.

So we trooped back upstairs. Pete was about to crank out a hundred copies of the flier, when I remembered something.

"Wait," I said. "We forgot to ask Lizzie if she wants to be in on this. Let me call her."

"What'd she say?" Termite asked when I came back to Pete's room.

"It was funny. She said no, thanks, she didn't really want to. She sounded awfully . . . well, sort of smug, like she was hiding something. I wonder what she's up to."

"Oh, well," said Pete.

"Oh, well," said Termite.

Pete began cranking. When his arms gave out, Termite took over. When Termite's arms gave out, I took over. It seemed to take forever, but finally we had one hundred copies.

"I'm starved," I announced after the fliers were divided into three even, neat stacks. "Let's stop for lunch."

Termite and I were just heading out the front door for our

own houses when Mrs. Wilson stopped us and invited us to
have sloppy joes with Pete, so of course we stayed.

After that, Termite and I were almost too full to move, but
Pete was hopping impatiently around the kitchen. Finally he
ran upstairs, got the fliers, brought them back down, and told
Termite and me the only way to get over feeling full was to
deliver all the fliers. So we groaned and got going.

Out on the sidewalk, Pete handed out the piles of fliers.
"For starters," he said, "Mac, you take our street, Termite,
you take Random Road, and I'll take Overbrook. Put a flier
in every mailbox, O.K.?"

So we did, and it went much faster than I expected. I got
rid of all thirty-three of my fliers before I'd finished our street.
When the three of us met up, we decided to crank out another
hundred. We delivered all those, too. It was almost four o'clock
before we finished. We were feeling pretty proud of ourselves.

In fact, we were feeling so good that when we were walking
up my driveway and Mom stopped us and said she and Dad
wanted to go shopping, we immediately volunteered to take
James to the school playground. Well, actually, Pete and I
said we'd do it. Termite suddenly decided to go home.

Mom handed James over to us with all sorts of instructions.
"Make sure he keeps his mittens on. And his hat. And he's
started eating gravel lately, so watch him. He's very subtle
about it. We're just going over to the shopping center. I think
Lizzie's going with you. If you have any trouble call Mrs.
Wilson. She's home, isn't she, Pete?" Pete nodded. "And
remember to check James's diaper. I just changed it, but that
doesn't mean anything."

James had been toilet-trained before he stopped talking, but
he wasn't anymore. He was back in diapers.

"Oh, and Jonno—" my mother started to say.

"Mom," I broke in, "we'll take care of him. Everything will be O.K."

She smiled at me. "I know. O.K. Thanks, kids. Mr. Peterson and I appreciate this."

We waved good-bye, and Dad backed the car out of the driveway.

Pete and I each took one of James's hands, and Lizzie got her red bike out of the garage. We walked slowly down the driveway and turned onto the sidewalk. James was trying to twist his hands out of ours and was weee-ooohing softly.

Lizzie caught up with us and rode slowly ahead while Pete and I struggled along with James. After a while, James calmed down a little. Pete and I discussed Time-Savers, and James hummed to himself and made funny little clucking sounds with his tongue.

"Hurry up!" Lizzie yelled impatiently. She was about four phone poles ahead of us, circling her bike in the street.

"We're trying to," I yelled back. "And get out of the middle of the road."

Lizzie coasted to the curb and rode on so slowly her bike teetered from side to side.

Finally we reached the playground. Even though the weather wasn't too great, a big bunch of kids were playing there, maybe twenty or so from the neighborhood, laughing and shouting, swinging, climbing on the monkey bars, riding the merry-go-round, hanging upside down on the jungle gym.

Lizzie parked her bike in a hurry and ran to the jungle gym, her favorite thing on the whole playground. Pete and I took James over to a swing and sat him on it. Pete pushed him and I stood in front of him, trying to get him to smile each time he swung toward me, but his face was solemn. He wasn't even looking at me. A couple of times he shouted "Weee-oooh!"

and flapped one of his hands vigorously. Three little kids in the sandbox watched him, looked at each other, and began to giggle.

"O.K., James, that's it for now," I said casually, grabbing his feet as he came forward, and easing him to a stop.

We took him to the slide next, pushed him down a few times, then played with him on the seesaw. By the time we sat him on the merry-go-round, he was getting antsy and whiny. When he began squirming tensely, I knew it was time to leave.

"We'd better go home," I said to Pete. "Where's Lizzie?"

We turned to scan the playground—and when we turned back, James was gone.

"Pete!" I shouted. "Where is he?"

We looked around frantically.

"I don't see him!" I said, shouting again, panic rising in me.

"Now just keep cool, Mac. There's Lizzie, still on the jungle gym. I'll go get her, and the three of us will spread out and look for James."

"O.K.," I said.

Pete ran off. The jungle gym was clear on the other side of the playground.

I stood where I was and started searching with my eyes. I climbed up on the merry-go-round for a little added height and looked at all the kids on the swings, the slide, the monkey bars, and in the sandbox.

No James.

Then I noticed a little crowd gathered near the drinking fountain. Something told me to go investigate, even though I knew I was supposed to wait for Pete and Lizzie.

I tore over to the crowd. Before I reached it, I heard one little kid shout gleefully, "Ew! He's eating gravel. Gross!"

Another one giggled and said, "He's taking his pants off!" *James.* Darn him.

All the kids were laughing and pointing.

Making fun of James.

I barged through the crowd, not sure what I was going to do.

There was James in the middle of a full-blown temper tantrum. His face was red from screaming, and he was making a funny noise that sounded like a goose honking. But worst of all, he'd somehow taken off his clothes right down to his diaper. Don't ask me how, when he won't dress himself for anything.

I stood glaring at all those giggling, pointing kids and felt I should yell at them—or do something. They were giggling at *me* now, as much as at James. But I couldn't say a thing. I couldn't open my mouth.

Maybe my glaring was enough, though. Suddenly I realized the kids were quiet. Not one of them said a word. They didn't apologize or offer to help me, but they had stopped giggling. They watched me silently. A couple of the kids in back drifted away.

I turned to James, angry at him, angry at the kids, angry at myself, and grabbed his arm, jerking it into the sleeve of his shirt. For just a second he looked surprised and hurt. Then his eyes glazed over and he weee-ooohed softly. It was almost a moan.

I finished dressing him as fast as I could, marched him past the few remaining children, and ran directly into Pete and Lizzie.

"Where were you?" Pete demanded accusingly.

Lizzie looked troubled and began to edge away from us.

"It doesn't matter," I said through clenched teeth. "I found

James, didn't I? Let's get out of here."

Lizzie and Pete knew something was wrong, but they didn't ask any questions. Lizzie just made a beeline for her bike and sped home ahead of us.

Pete and I were silent on the way back, and I was grateful for that. I knew we weren't really mad at each other and that we'd patch things up later.

As for James, I could have clobbered him. I'd never been so embarrassed in my life. But clobbering him wouldn't have done much good.

James didn't understand anything.

6. Monkey-in-the-Middle

On Monday morning, Termite and Pete and I were sitting around on the desks in our classroom as usual. Most of the kids in the class had already arrived. Elise and the gang were in, and so were Steph and Claud. For some odd reason all the in-boys were missing. Edweird hadn't arrived yet, but he didn't usually get in until right before the second bell.

Pete and Termite and I were talking about Time-Savers, trying to figure out what to do if one of us started getting more jobs than the others, when suddenly there was this commotion in the front of the room. Termite stopped talking, and the three of us looked up to see Chris, Alan, Hank, and Dave standing in a row by Mr. Westoff's desk. Alan was holding a piece of paper, and the four of them were reading aloud from it in unison, like they were reciting a poem or something.

"Baby-sitting," they were saying, "pet-sitting, cleaning, gardening, window washing, lawn mowing..."

The list went on and on. Our list.

They had one of our Time-Savers fliers. And they were making it sound really dumb and babyish. Elise, Janie, Louise, and Margaret were practically rolling in the aisles.

The boys started this stupid play.

"Oh, Mr. Giancossi," Hank said, "I'll do anything for you. Anything at all."

"O.K., Jonathan," said Chris to Hank, and I could feel my face burning. "I need someone to clean out our sewer, but I can only pay ten cents an hour."

"Oh, that's fine, sir, just fine," said Hank in this squeaky voice. He made me sound like a girl.

Then they went back to reading the rest of our ad, complete with our names and phone numbers.

Everyone was laughing. Even Steph and Claud looked like they were going to break down any minute. I couldn't blame them.

Just as the boys started reading the last line, Pete jumped off his desk and ran to Alan. "Give me that!" he shouted, grabbing for the paper.

Alan swiped it out of his reach, crumpled it up, and tossed it to Dave, who had run to the other side of the room.

Pete ran to Dave, his face beet-red. "I said give me that!"

Dave tossed it to Chris.

It was monkey-in-the-middle, and Pete was the monkey.

"Forget it, Pete," Termite was saying.

I sat down on my chair. I couldn't look at anybody.

Pete gave up and came back to us. None of us said a word. But I felt better when Steph and Claud wandered over and Claud said, "I bet they're just jealous because they didn't have a good idea like that."

I knew it wasn't true, but it was nice of her to say it.

Then suddenly the room went dead-silent. I looked up, expecting to see the vice-principal in the doorway. Instead I saw Edweird. So did everybody else. We were all staring.

Edweird was decked out in a red-and-white checked shirt,

huge blue jeans, a beaded belt, cowboy boots, and a cowboy hat.

For just a few seconds, our whole class was frozen. Nobody spoke or moved.

"Howdy, podners," said Edweird into the silence.

Oh, Edweird, I thought. Now you've done it.

Alan was the first to unfreeze. He snorted. "Howdy," he said sarcastically.

Edweird hooked his thumbs in his jeans pockets. "Flew to a ranch this weekend," he drawled. It was a pretty good drawl, but no one seemed too impressed. "My uncle's," he went on.

"Rope any cows?" asked Chris, with barely concealed hysteria.

The class was ready to explode with laughter. I could feel it. It was like pressure building, but everyone was hanging on longer than usual. I think we were all remembering Mr. Westoff's talk last Monday. We knew Chris wasn't supposed to be teasing Edweird, and we knew we shouldn't laugh at him. Mr. Westoff had explained that Edweird wasn't retarded but that he had severe emotional problems. The problems kept him from doing well in school, and they made him act different. He didn't know how to behave around people, and he didn't know how to make friends. So we were supposed to be nice to him. Especially since he'd just moved to our town and this was the first time he was trying out a regular classroom, and the teachers and school officials and especially Edweird wanted it to work.

So we were holding in the laughter. Most of us, at any rate. I heard a few giggles leaking from Janie and Louise.

And then Dave, forgetting everything, came out and said how could Edweird have ridden a horse, he was so fat. The rest of the laughter escaped at last.

Even my own. Even when I saw Edweird's hurt, stunned face as he hung his head and sat down at his desk.

And, I suppose, in order to worm my way back into Chris's good graces after the Time-Savers thing, I said that probably the only horse Edweird could ride was on a merry-go-round.

A couple of minutes later, the first bell rang. Termite made a beeline for his classroom, and Mr. Westoff came in. We weren't much noisier than usual by that time, and he never knew what had happened. He just shot Edweird a curious look when he headed for the Resource Room in his cowboy suit.

All day in school I felt pretty bad about what we'd done to Edweird (and about what the in-kids had done to Termite and Pete and me), but I forgot about everything as soon as I got home.

This was because I heard from the E-Z Seed Company. I opened the letter fast, wondering where the seeds were.

The letter said:

Dear Mr. Peterson:
The E-Z Seed Company is pleased that you want to join its nationwide sales force. At the moment we are processing your application. Within several days you will receive 300 packages of vegetable and flower seeds, and complete instructions for proceeding with the venture.
Congratulations, Mr. Peterson!
Yours truly,
Melvin Chamberlain
President, E-Z Seed Company

I read the letter over a few times.

Wow! *Mr*. Peterson, venture, sales force, nationwise, president. This must be something really big.

I'd just gotten to "proceeding with the venture" for the fourth time when—*CRASH*. A huge thump came from upstairs, followed by the sound of glass breaking, by one of James's more angry shrieks, and by my mother shouting, "James! Bad boy!" She sounded pretty angry herself.

I raced upstairs in time to see James galloping down the hallway toward his room. He was hopping-mad about something. He kept screaming over and over again, not even weeeooohing, just screaming.

As I reached the top step, Mom bolted out of the bathroom in pursuit of James, hesitated briefly when she saw me, and then continued down the hall.

"What's going on?" I shouted. I tore after them.

I reached James's room and found him throwing a temper tantrum. He was jumping up and down, screaming to beat the band, and hitting his face with his fists.

Mom seemed paralyzed by the whole thing, so I dashed in and grabbed James's fists. The last time he hit himself like this, he left bruises all over his face. He even gave himself a black eye.

James screamed louder when I grabbed him, but I didn't let go. I just stood there and held his hands. Finally he wore himself out. The screaming and jumping stopped and he was still, gazing up at the ceiling light. Very slowly I loosened my grip and let go of his hands. They were limp. He sank down to the floor, lost in his own world.

I turned around to see Mom leaning against the doorjamb, crying silently. The tears were running down her cheeks, and she wasn't trying to stop them. She reminded me of a battery that had worn out. Suddenly she didn't have the energy to react to anything. It was as if James had finally gotten the best of her.

"What happened?" I asked. I was shaking. James scares me

to death when he does that. He acts like a little wild animal.

"Oh," said Mom, tiredly, "he was in the bathroom spinning pennies—don't ask me why; he hasn't done that in weeks, but he's been doing it all day today—and I went in to change his diaper. As soon as I touched him, he got angry. He jumped up, knocked over the wastebasket, grabbed it, and threw it. It broke the mirror."

Mom sounded so tired.

"I really don't know," she said finally, wiping the tears away, "how much more of this I can take."

We tiptoed out of James's room, hoping he'd stay quiet in there for a while.

"Mom," I said, "why don't you call the school? Maybe they'll have some suggestions or something."

"I guess. All right. Thanks, Jonno," she said. "I'm going to go in the bedroom to make the call, and then I don't want to be disturbed for a while, O.K.?"

"O.K. I'll tell Lizzie when she gets home."

Mom closed the bedroom door softly.

I went back to James's room and looked in. He was sitting cross-legged on the floor where we'd left him. He was rocking back and forth, saying a brand-new sound over and over again. "Oh-*ma,* oh-*ma,* oh-*ma.*"

I wondered if I'd ever know what he meant.

7. Good News

I locked James in his room and considered cleaning up the mess in the bathroom, but decided maybe Dad could do it for once. I didn't see why I should get stuck with so many of James's messes.

Then I went downstairs to start my homework. Mr. Westoff had been pretty easy on us. I only had two pages of math review to do. I finished them just as Lizzie got home.

"Hi," I said as she came in the door. "Where've you been?"

"I stayed late to get some help from my art teacher."

"Art teacher? Help with what?"

"Can't tell you." Lizzie crossed her arms and smiled at me. She was being smug again.

"Come on."

"Nope."

"Well, want to come outside with me? I just finished my homework." Lizzie hardly ever had any.

"Nope," she said again. "I have to go work on something."

I looked at her suspiciously. "Well, be quiet upstairs. Mom's resting. . . . But everything's O.K.," I added quickly.

"Where's James?" she asked.

"In his room. But I think I'll go get him and take him outside."

So I did, and he was much calmer. We fooled around in the front yard. In a little while Pete came over, and we tried to teach James to catch the basketball, but it was hopeless. James darted all over the place, never looking at us or the ball, so of course he couldn't catch it. Finally Pete and I got silly. We were lying on the grass laughing when Mom and Lizzie came out and sat on the front porch.

Mom looked terrific, considering. She was smiling and didn't seem at all tired. That nap or whatever had worked wonders. I guess we all had a little spring fever because suddenly we were in good moods.

Then Dad got home early, which put us in an even better mood. He never comes home early.

"Dad!" I cried as he was parking the car. "What's going on?"

"What do you mean?" he asked cheerfully, easing himself out from behind the steering wheel. "It's a beautiful spring day, that's all." He slammed the door shut.

Mrs. Wilson called Pete in then.

"See you," I yelled to him as he ran home.

Dad strode across the front lawn, kissed Mom and Lizzie, and patted James on the head.

James ducked away from him and squealed, "Oh-*ma*."

"Where'd *that* come from?" asked my father. "I never heard that before."

"Who knows?" I said. "It's new."

"Funny," said Dad.

"Well, let's all go in and have dinner," suggested Mom.

With everybody (everybody except James, of course) working happily, we threw together a gigantic chef's salad in record time. Mom heated up a quiche in the oven.

We sat at the table and were about to start dishing out the food when Mom said, "Let's say grace."

We don't say grace too often. We're not very religious. We don't even go to church. But every now and then we give thanks for what we have. We have our own way of doing it. First we join hands.

"O.K., Dad, you start," I said. We always start with the oldest in the family.

"I want to give thanks for this beautiful day, and for my family, whom I love very much." He smiled across the table at my mother. "I'm thankful we're here together."

Mom was next. "I want to give thanks for some wonderful news I received this afternoon. I'll tell you about it after grace."

"Oh, no fair!" groaned Lizzie. "I can't wait."

"My lips are sealed," Mom said, grinning. "O.K., Jonno. Now you."

I thought a minute. "I'm thankful for my family and my friends, and I'm thankful it's baseball season."

Lizzie's turn. "I'm thankful for my friends, too," she said. I wondered what she meant, considering she hardly had any friends.

"Oh-*ma*," cried James suddenly. We looked at him almost as if we expected *him* to give thanks.

Mom cleared her throat. "Well," she said, "my good news concerns James."

Dad started serving the quiche and salad and passing around the plates. "James?" he asked Mom. "What is it?"

"Well, we had a little scene with him this afternoon. By-the-way-the-bathroom-mirror-is-broken-and-we'll-have-to-re-place-it," she said in a rush, getting that part over with quickly, before Dad could get angry. "So I called Dr. Wyman, the

director of the Weston Child Development Institute, and explained that James was getting out of hand, and guess what
he said."

"What?" we all asked, leaning toward her.

"That starting Monday James can go to school for half
days—"

"Yay!" I cheered.

"—and that by mid-April they'll have an opening and he
can go for full days."

"Hey, that's really something to celebrate," said Dad. "Just
a second." He jumped up, went into the kitchen, and came
back with a bottle of wine and two wineglasses.

He and Mom toasted each other and James and his future.

During dinner, Mom explained some stuff to us. It turned
out we were all going to be involved in James's program.
Lizzie didn't look too happy about this.

"How do you mean?" I asked.

"Yeah," said Lizzie, "how do you mean?"

"Now, just a second," said Mom. "I don't like the tone of
your voices. I know that having a brother like James makes
great demands on you two, but if we want to help him, we're
going to have to do our parts. James can't do it alone, or even
with just his teacher's help. He's a little boy, and he needs
us."

I looked over at James, who, for the moment, was solemnly
eating a bagel without ever looking at it. He was peaceful now,
but I knew it wouldn't last. He sat and hummed, gazing off
somewhere, far away from the dining room. It had been a few
days since we'd tried to force anything healthy down him,
which I knew wasn't good. We were starting to give up. I
knew he needed the school; I just hadn't counted on having
much to do with it.

"Of course," my mother continued, "I can't force you to

help James, but the more help he gets, the faster he'll change. So before you decide not to help, why don't I tell you what it will involve."

"O.K.," Lizzie and I said hesitantly.

James screamed suddenly, threw down his bagel, and tried to struggle out of his highchair.

"You might find it interesting," put in Dad, unbuckling James and letting him go. "When your mother and I first spoke to Dr. Wyman, I was concerned about what he expected us to do at home, too, but when I understood how it all worked, I felt differently."

James ran over to a Lincoln Logs project in the living room.

"What we'll be most involved with," began my mother, "is making sure James keeps up at home the things he's learning in school."

"I don't get it," said Lizzie.

"Well, James's school is not like yours. You and Jonno learn reading and writing and math and spelling. But James has a lot to learn before he can ever *begin* those things. He has to learn to eat properly, to use the bathroom, to dress himself, to play, not to have tantrums, and most important, to talk. The school's going to start teaching him those things right away. And James is probably not going to like it one bit. Nobody likes to be asked to change. It would be just as if I got up one morning and said, 'Lizzie, from now on, you have to crawl on your hands and knees instead of walk, and Jonno, you're going to have to learn to eat cabbage three times a day.'"

"Ick," said Lizzie.

"Gross," said I.

"Now, James is going to think he only has to do these new things at school where he's learning them," continued Mom, "but we'll want him to do them at home, right?"

"Right."

"And that's why we'll have to pay close attention to what Dr. Wyman tells us. If we start getting lazy and letting him eat bagels sometimes or wear diapers sometimes, James will be confused. He won't know what we expect of him, and he'll think we're not serious about what we're teaching him—that eventually he can go back to the way he is now."

"Oh, I see," said Lizzie slowly.

"You mean we have to be consistent, right?" I asked.

"Exactly," said my mother, smiling.

We were quiet for a moment, thinking everything over.

"Mom, Dad," I said finally, "I'll help, I guess, but I have one question."

"Shoot," said Dad.

"What if James is happy the way he is now? Why should we decide to change him? Maybe it's not fair. Just like it wouldn't be fair if I did suddenly have to eat cabbage three times a day. I'm happy now. Why should anyone change me? It's my life and nobody else's."

Mom and Dad looked at each other, and at me. Lizzie eyed me from under the baseball cap, frowning.

"That's a very important question, Jonno," Mom said quietly. "And the only answer I have is that maybe it's *not* fair to ask James to change. Maybe we don't have the right. But if we have to continue the way we're living now, I don't think I can handle it. And the alternative would be to put James in an institution, because we can't afford a residential school for him the rest of his life. What it boils down to is either we ask James to change or we put him away."

We were quiet again for a few seconds.

Finally Lizzie let out a long sigh. "I always wanted to be a teacher," she said.

During the rest of dinner, Mom and Dad explained how we would be involved in James's schooling. Family members were encouraged to visit the school and watch James and his teachers as often as possible. Starting Monday, Mom would spend as many mornings there as she could, and Dad would try to get away from the office at least twice a week to do the same. They wanted Lizzie and me to visit, too, but not until our spring vacation, when we'd be out of school and James wouldn't.

Then Mom explained about home visits. "Dr. Wyman and one of James's teachers will come to our house in the evening now and then. They want to meet us—"

"Why?" interrupted Lizzie.

"I guess so they can understand James better. When somebody won't talk, you don't get to know much about him, and it's harder to help him. But if you meet the people in his family and see how he lives, then, well, you know him a little better."

"Also," said Dad, "they'll want to see if James's behavior at school is the same as it is at home. What if James doesn't have tantrums at school? Then Dr. Wyman will have to come here to see them. He can't help us handle them unless he sees them."

"And," said Mom, "when Dr. Wyman visits, we'll have time to ask all the questions we want. You and Lizzie, especially. It'll be a time to speak your minds, to say whether things about James's work are bothering you, or if you've noticed anything new he's doing, or if you want advice about how to handle him. Anything at all."

I was mulling all this over when the phone rang. "I'll get it!" I shouted, jumping up from the table and running into the kitchen.

"Hello?" I said when I'd picked up the receiver.

"Hello, I'd like to speak to Jonathan Peterson," said an unfamiliar voice. It sounded like a grown-up. A woman.

"This is Jonathan."

"Hi Jonathan. My name is Mrs. Rice. I live up on Random Road. I got your Time-Savers ad?" She made it a question.

"Oh, yes," I said. "Can I help you?" I tried to sound calm even though I was so excited, I had a whole fleet of butterflies in my stomach.

"Yes," she said, "I need someone to paint the fence around our garbage cans. It's not a very big fence. I think you could do it in an afternoon. Are you interested?"

"Sure! I can come tomorrow. Is tomorrow O.K.?"

"It's fine."

I got all the details about the time and the address, and then called Pete and gave him the good news. It turned out he'd gotten a Time-Savers call, too—from a very odd-sounding person who wanted him to clean out his sewers for ten cents an hour. It was Chris, of course. We grumbled to each other about it for a while.

By the time I got off the phone, dinner was over, and Dad and Lizzie were cleaning up. I went into the living room, expecting to find Mom reading to James, but James was alone, sitting on the floor. Only when I came in, he looked directly into my eyes. Then he stood up and walked over to me.

"Oh-*ma*," he said, putting his hand on my knee.

"James?" I asked.

I sat down on the couch and James sat next to me all by himself. I put my arm around him and we stayed quietly like that until I realized he was lost to the ceiling light again.

I pulled my arm away and called his name, but he didn't move.

James, I thought, I don't understand you at all.

8. E-Z Seeds

When I got home from school Thursday afternoon, Mom greeted me at the door with a big box. "Look what came in the mail for you today, sweetie. It's from the E-Z Seed Company."

"Oh, wow!" I cried. "That was fast! I can't believe it!"

"What was fast? What is it?" asked Mom.

We sat down at the kitchen table. I could see James in the living room hovering around a half-finished Lincoln Logs project.

"I'm going to sell seeds, Mom," I said. "I've got two ways to earn money now. Time-Savers and seed-selling."

"That's great, Jonno. I'm really proud of you."

On Tuesday I'd earned $3.75 painting Mrs. Rice's garbage can fence, and today I'd earn $10.00 selling eight packages of seeds, and then I'd have $13.75 toward the Starcruiser, which was more than one-fifth of the total price.

"How'd you get those seeds?" asked Mom curiously.

I told her how the E-Z Seed Company worked.

"Hmmm," was all she said.

"What is it? I can tell something's wrong." Sometimes Mom could spoil everything. She was such a worrier.

"Nothing," she said slowly.

"I'm going out right now," I said, leaping up and heading off with my box.

"Don't you want anything to eat?"

"No, thanks, I don't have time."

I took the box up to my room, tore it open, scanned the directions to make certain I knew what I was doing, dumped the seeds in a paper bag, and started off down our street.

The first house I went to was the Marshalls'. They are our next-door neighbors. It wasn't until I was walking up their front path that I began to wonder what I should say when somebody answered the door. Then I began hoping Taylor Marshall wouldn't answer the door. He was sixteen and this neat football player. Maybe he'd think seed-selling was babyish.

I almost turned away to go to another house, but I remembered the Starcruiser. Besides it was only a little after three o'clock. A high school football star would probably be out on the field, practicing dropkicks or something.

So I drew in a big breath and rang the bell.

Taylor answered it.

It never fails.

He must have been home sick, because he was wearing his robe and these old threadbare pajamas.

I'd probably gotten him out of bed for my dumb seeds.

"Hey, sport." He grinned. "What's doing?"

"Hi," I said weakly. "Is—um—is your mother home?"

"Nope. She's off driving Sam's piano lesson car pool. Can I give her a message?"

"Well..." I began. *Now* what was I supposed to do? Obviously I was there for a reason. "Well," I said again, stalling for time.

Taylor began to look a little impatient. "Yeah?"

I took the plunge. "I'm selling these seeds," I said as fast as possible, "and I was wondering if you wanted to buy any. They're from a very respectable place. But I can come back another time."

"That would probably be a good idea," said Taylor, and for some reason I felt relieved. "I don't know what Mom and Dad want to do. About gardens, I mean. Why don't you come back in an hour or so?"

"O.K. No problem." I backed down the steps, shouted "Thanks," and ran across the side lawn to the Franklins' house.

Mr. and Mrs. Franklin are real old and very nice, even if they are a little deaf. I rang the bell and waited forever. Just as I was about to give up, Mr. Franklin opened the door.

"Hi, there!" he said in this loud, hearty voice, but he didn't fool me. I knew perfectly well he didn't have the vaguest idea who I was.

"Hi, Mr. Franklin," I yelled, hoping his hearing aid was connected. *"I'm selling seeds."*

"You're collecting weeds? What is it, a science project or something? Well, my goodness, there are enough weeds out there to eat a horse." (Mr. Franklin sometimes gets his words mixed up.) "Go on. Take whatever you need." He gestured out across his front lawn.

"No, Mr. Franklin," I shouted. *"I'm SELLING SEEDS."* I opened the bag and showed him the packages. *"Do you want to buy any?"*

"Selling them, are you?" he asked.

I nodded.

"Well, let's have a look. Come on inside, son."

I followed him into the living room. It was dark and smelled funny. Sort of like lavender and spices and perfume all mixed up. I wondered how you could live with a smell like that. Maybe the Franklins' hearing wasn't the only thing that was fading. I tried to breathe through my mouth.

Mrs. Franklin was sitting in the living room reading. When she saw me, she took off her glasses and folded them neatly in her lap.

"Hello there, Jonathan," she said in her quiet voice.

"Hi, Mrs. Franklin."

"This young man is selling seeds, Mother," said Mr. Franklin.

"He's felling trees?"

"No, he's *selling seeds*."

I'd tell you the rest of the conversation, but it went on like that forever.

By the time I left the Franklins' it was almost four o'clock, and I'd sold them exactly one package of seeds.

Petunias.

In my pocket was fifty cents.

I got to keep twelve-and-a-half cents of it.

I had a long, long, long way to go before I hit ten dollars.

However, maybe the Franklins were unusual. And after all, I could still go back to the Marshalls'. Later. If felt like it.

The house next door to the Franklins' was the Steinwicks'. As in Alan Steinwick. No way was I going in there. I didn't want to go through the Time-Savers routine again with the in-boys. I didn't even dare to cut across Alan's front lawn. I detoured down to the sidewalk and made my way to the Valentines' house.

I rang the bell. No answer.

I went on to the Cornwalls'. Mrs. Cornwall said that no, thank you, she most certainly did not care to buy any seeds. And that was that.

I checked my watch: 4:10.

I pressed on.

I didn't know the people next to the Cornwalls, but it didn't matter. A woman answered the door and was delighted to see a seed-seller standing on her front stoop.

"This is perfect!" she cried. "I was just planning my vegetable garden. Do you have carrot seeds?"

I nodded.

"Green peppers?"

I nodded.

"Corn?"

I nodded.

I had everything she wanted. In the end she bought ten packets. Five dollars, and I got to keep a dollar twenty-five. That was more like it!

At the next two houses nobody was home.

I'd reached the end of our street. It was time to hit the homes on the other side.

I rang the door at the Phomalonts'. Dr. Phomalont is my doctor. Her husband answered the door.

"Well, Jonathan! Nice to see you!"

"Hi, Mr. Phomalont," I said smiling. I like him a lot.

"I'm selling seeds," I said, suddenly feeling sort of important.

"Well, now, what have you got?"

I showed him. He bought five packages of flower seeds. He was very nice about it, but I had the funny feeling he didn't *really* need them. Not like the lady who wanted the vegetables. I headed next door, to the Jordans.

Since both Mr. and Mrs. Jordan work, a maid comes in to take care of their three children. Her name is Rosa. She doesn't speak a whole lot of English.

When I rang the doorbell, I could hear some yelling going on inside, and a stampede to get to the door.

"I'll get it!" called a high little voice.

"No, I'll get it!"

"No, I'll—"

Thump, crash. I think there was a pile-up on the other side of the door.

Then a very firm voice said, "No, *I* get it." That was Rosa. The door opened about a quarter of an inch.

"Hello?" I said.

"Hello?" said Rosa.

"Hello, my name is Jonathan Eckhardt Peterson, and I'm selling seeds. I was wondering if—"

"Hello?"

I started over again.

"Let *me* see, Rosie," came an impatient voice. The door jerked open a few inches. "What are you selling?" It was Teddy, the oldest of the kids. He was James's age and talking in sentences and everything.

"Seeds, Teddy," I said. "Want to see?"

Teddy squirmed his way between Rosa and the door.

"What? What you sell? You sell something?" asked Rosa suspiciously. She elbowed herself in front of Teddy. Teddy dropped to his hands and knees and tried to crawl out.

I began to feel fidgety. I reached into my bag and pulled out a handful of seed packets, starting in on my little talk again.

But before I got halfway through, Rosa suddenly cried, "No! No selling! No selling! Good-bye!" She slammed the door.

I gave up and went home. It was growing dark anyway.

I must have looked pretty discouraged when I entered our house.

Mom, James, and Lizzie were all sitting around in the living room.

"What hap— How did you do, dear?" asked Mom carefully, as I plopped down on the floor next to Lizzie.

"Well...not great and not bad. But I'm already running

out of houses to go to. I mean, there're only a few more streets in this neighborhood, and I didn't make that much money today. Nowhere near the ten dollars I was expecting to earn. I don't know if it's worth it. Plus, I get the feeling some people don't like salesmen at their doors."

"I'll buy some seeds," said Lizzie. Mom must have explained my project to her.

"Thanks," I said, "but you have to save your money. It's O.K., anyway. I think I'm finished with E-Z Seeds."

"Listen, Jonno, before I forget," said Mom. "Pete called a few minutes ago. He wants you to call back. He sounded excited."

"Oh, good," I said without any enthusiasm, and headed for the phone. I dialed his number. "Pete? It's me."

"Mac! Great news! A Time-Saver job. Get this. Mrs. Schwartz on Overbrook Drive called a little while ago, and she needs two baby-sitters for all Saturday afternoon. She'll pay us *each* a dollar fifty an hour. That's seven fifty apiece! Termite's gonna be away this weekend, so do you want to take the job with me?"

"Sure!" I cried.

"Good. We have to be there at one o'clock sharp. Meet me at my house at twelve forty-five and we'll walk over together."

"O.K. . . . Pete?"

"Yeah?"

"How come the Schwartzes need *two* baby-sitters?"

There was a pause at Pete's end. A loud pause, if you know what I mean.

"Well," he said at last, "because there're going to be eight children to take care of."

I almost dropped the receiver. *"Eight?* But the Schwartzes only have four."

"I know. Their cousins will be visiting."

"Aw, Pete."

"Listen, it's only five hours. And it's seven fifty. You can handle it, can't you?"

"Sure. I guess so."

But I wasn't sure at all.

9. The Baby-sitting Disaster

That Thursday was the end of my E-Z seed-selling. It hadn't been E-Z at all. I figured I earned more money per hour on Time-Savers jobs, and didn't risk angry maids yelling at me either. So I took the 278 leftover seed packs, and the $8.25 the E-Z people earned from the $11.00, and wrapped them up to return to the company.

Mom came into my room as I was finishing. "The seeds?" she asked, watching me write out the label.

"Yeah."

"I wanted to tell you this afternoon that those mail order moneymaking businesses are usually not as profitable or as easy to carry out as they're advertised. But I thought you should have the chance to find out for yourself. Who knows? You might have been a supersalesman."

I smiled at her. "The ad made it sound so terrific. It said you could earn as much as ten dollars a day. They shouldn't be allowed to lie like that."

"Well, unfortunately, they weren't lying. The key words in that ad are *could*—that only means *might*— and *as much as*— that only means anything *up to* ten dollars. You just have to learn to watch out for things like that. Adults get misled by advertisements, too. I'm sorry you had to learn this lesson the hard way, but it wasn't all bad. At least you earned a little money. Now you can forget about the whole thing."

"Yeah," I said again.

Mom watched me finish the label and paste it on the box. "I'll take that to the post office for you tomorrow."

"Thanks," I said. "I don't ever want to see another E-Z seed as long as I live."

Mom grinned at me. "Precisely how I feel about Crack-up Crackers."

"About what?"

"Crack-up Crackers—a joke in every box. I spent all afternoon writing ads for them. You should hear the jokes. They're terrible."

"Like what?"

"What's big and red and eats rocks?"

"I give up."

"A big, red rock-eater."

"Yeah?"

"That's it. A big, red rock-eater."

"That's it? That's the joke?"

"Mm-hmmm." Mom was hiding a smile.

"Sheesh."

We both burst out laughing.

On Saturday I turned up at Pete's at exactly twelve forty-five. He came out the front door before I could even ring the bell.

"Ready?" he asked.

"I hope so."

Mrs. Schwartz seemed awfully glad to see us. We were five

minutes early. "Thank goodness you're here so soon," she exclaimed.

I glanced nervously at Pete. That was not a good sign.

She let us in. The place was a madhouse. People everywhere, but mostly in the living room. There were Mr. and Mrs. Schwartz, their four kids, the four cousins, and their four parents, plus a few more stray aunts and uncles, a grandmother, I think, and Woof, the Schwartz's sheepdog. While Pete and I tried to take all this in, Mrs. Schwartz began the introductions.

"You already know Polly, Andy, Frankie, and Lissa," she said, pointing out the four Schwartzes. Those she could find, at any rate. She couldn't see Andy and Lissa, but it didn't matter because I could. They were wearing pig hats and were tearing up the stairs to the second floor, oinking and grunting and slurping.

Then she pointed out the youngest of the whole crowd—a chubby baby seated on the floor. He didn't look like he could walk yet, thank goodness.

"That's Joey," she said. "And don't worry about him at all. He's due for a nap any minute. He'll sleep all afternoon. He's Mr. Schwartz's brother's baby. The other three, Mr. Schwartz's other brother's children, are Cindy"—she pointed to a little girl about two years old—"Michael"—she pointed to a boy about James's age who had just dumped all the pieces to six jigsaw puzzles in one large heap on the floor—"and Adrienne"—she pointed to a girl Lizzie's age who was playing with little Joey. Adrienne looked like she was the oldest of the passle of kids.

At that moment Woof, who had been hanging around in the kitchen, hiding out from the chaos, came bounding into the living room, whuffling and whining.

"And that's Woof," added Mrs. Schwartz. "He wants his kibbles. I'll feed him before we leave. By the way, Adrienne's cat, Persephone, is here, locked up in Polly and Lissa's room. And Marco Polo, Mrs. Divine's"—here Mrs. Schwartz indicated the grandmother-person—"cocker spaniel, is locked up in the laundry room. All the pets have to be kept separate. They don't know each other and won't get along. Oh, but don't worry about Persephone or Marco Polo. They don't have to be fed or anything. Just don't let them out."

Mrs. Schwartz went on a mile a minute. My head was swimming. Even Pete was looking slightly nervous.

It turned out the adults were going to a wedding. While they were gone we were supposed to:

> Entertain Adrienne (8), Polly (7), Andy (5), Michael (5), Lissa (4), Cindy (2), and Frankie (2). Joey, apparently, really was going to nap—but until six o'clock? At any rate he had been put in Frankie's crib and was quiet.
> Keep the pets separated.
> Give the seven older kids a snack at three o'clock.

Mrs. Schwartz had left a long list of emergency numbers and told us the next-door neighbors would be home all afternoon. She'd also left out a can of Hawaiian Punch and a box of Ritz Crackers for the three-o'clock snack.

I breathed a sigh of relief when the wedding posse took off. Even though it meant Pete and I were left alone with all the kids, it cut the number of people in the house down by eleven.

As soon as the adults got out the front door, Cindy and Frankie started crying. Loudly.

"I want Mommy," they wailed in unison.

I looked at Pete. I hadn't encountered too much of this sort of thing. I don't think he had either.

Luckily for us, Adrienne came to the rescue. She carried a big Oscar the Grouch hand puppet over to them.

"Lookit this, Cindy. Look, Frankie. I'm Oscar the Grouch. Here's my garbage can." She stuck her hand in back of a wastebasket.

Cindy and Frankie looked pretty interested. Even so, they let their wails drag on awhile, like they didn't want to let go of them.

I checked out Michael, Polly, Andy, and Lissa on the other side of the living room. They were sitting around trying to straighten out Michael's jigsaw puzzle mess.

Well, was this it? Was this baby-sitting? It seemed so easy. Joey was asleep, four of the kids were entertaining each other, and Adrienne was entertaining two others. There wasn't even anything for Pete and me to do. Taking care of James was harder than this.

So I sat down with Adrienne and the little kids, and Pete sat down with the others, and we all played quietly until almost three o'clock.

Then we trooped into the kitchen for juice and crackers. There were no squabbles. Nobody even spilled anything. I couldn't believe it. Why are adults always complaining about how hard it is to be a parent?

I don't know exactly when Pete and I made our mistake. It may have been when we suggested that everybody play outside. The Schwartzes have a big fenced-in backyard with swings and monkey bars and a jungle gym. Lizzie would have loved it. But when we made the suggestion we got a chorus of no's.

Probably we should've left well enough alone, not pressed our luck. But to be honest, Pete and I were bored stiff with puzzles and Oscar the Grouch stories.

"Oh, come on," said Pete cheerfully. "I'll race everybody. Bet I can beat you all outside."

That did it.

I was almost trampled.

There was this explosion of energy, and seven small bodies, one larger one, and one shaggy, four-footed one scrambled and crashed down a flight of steps and out the back door.

I stood in the empty living room and listened.

Sure enough, Joey began to cry. I tiptoed upstairs, but just as I reached the top step, the crying stopped. I stood still, listening and counting. When I didn't hear a sound for twenty seconds, I turned around and went back downstairs and outside.

In the backyard the kids had gone wild. They were whooping and screeching and chasing each other. Woof was right in the middle of everything, leaping up and down. Pete looked desperate.

"Hey!" I shouted. "Hey!"

Nobody stopped, but Polly yelled back, "What?"

"Come here, everybody!"

"Why?"

"We're going to play Duck, Duck, Goose."

"Are you kidding?" yelped Adrienne. "Yuck. That's for babies."

"What's Duck, Duck, Goose?" asked Lissa.

Pete and I looked at each other and shrugged. I thought kids were born knowing how to play Duck, Duck, Goose.

"Forget it," I said.

They forgot. Cindy and Frankie climbed onto swings, and Pete and I pushed them while the older kids got in a huddle as far away from us as possible.

I nudged Pete. "Hey," I whispered. "Look at that."

Pete glanced over at the huddle and then back at me. "Yeah? So?"

"It looks suspicious. It looks like a plot."

"Geez, Mac, they're only little kids."

I didn't say anything.

In a minute or two, Polly left the huddle and came skipping over to us. "Want to play hide-and-seek?" she asked sweetly. She took Pete's hand. "Please, Pete?"

Pete smiled over at me as if to say, "Now isn't this nice? The children want to play a game after all. And you thought they were plotting...."

I shot Pete this smirk that I save for very rare occasions.

"Sure," Pete said, letting Polly lead him away.

"All right," I said reluctantly. I helped Cindy and Frankie off the swings. "You can play, too," I told them. "You can team up with Adrienne and Polly."

I trotted them over to the rest of the kids. Adrienne was giving directions.

"O.K., the person who's it goes in the toolshed and counts to a hundred." She pointed to a back corner of the yard where a brown wooden shed was partly hidden by some tall grass and a rhododendron bush.

"Why the toolshed?" I asked suspiciously.

Pete kicked my ankle and I kicked him back. He wasn't used to younger kids the way I was. I remembered the day Lizzie was so sweet to me because she'd left a dead garter snake in my bed.

"Why the toolshed?" repeated Adrienne slightly nervously. "Oh, just because...because then we don't have to worry about anyone peeking. You can't see out of the shed if the door's closed."

"Oh, all right," I sighed.

Something was going on.

"I'll be first," cried Adrienne.

"Take Cindy with you," I said. "You can be a team. And Polly, you be a team with Frankie."

"I'll count to fifty," Adrienne called, and opened the door.

Cindy just stood there.

"Go on, Cindy," said Adrienne.

Cindy shook her head.

"Yes," insisted Adrienne.

Cindy shook harder. "No. Not in the dark."

"I'll take her," I said. Anything to prevent tears. I wanted everyone to look happy when the mommies and daddies came back.

So Adrienne went in the shed and the rest of us scattered, looking for hiding spots. It wasn't easy finding one I could get Cindy in, as well. The little cousins seemed to know the yard inside out and scrambled up trees, under bushes, behind benches. By the time Adrienne burst through the door, Pete and Cindy and I were still standing around like a bunch of fools.

"You're it!" shouted Adrienne gleefully. "All-y-all-y in free!"

Everybody tumbled out of their hiding places and gathered around Adrienne, who was having a fit of giggles. "Pete and Jon couldn't even find places!" she managed to squeal. "Hee hee hee. They were standing right where I left them. Hee hee hee. Now they're it!"

"O.K., O.K.," I said crossly. "So we don't know the yard too well. Here, Adrienne. Take Cindy. *You* try finding a place big enough for two."

"I know lots," she said maddeningly, still laughing. "O.K., hee hee, now you two go in the shed."

"Sure, sure," said Pete. "Come on, Mac."

"I'll go with you," said Adrienne.

"You don't have to," I said.

But she came anyway, waited until Pete and I were well inside, and closed the door on us.

Then I heard a click. It sounded an awful lot like a lock turning. I rushed over to the door, grabbed the knob, and turned. Nothing. I shook the door. "Adrienne!" I yelled at the top of my lungs. "Open this door!"

"Hee hee hee."

"Geez, Pete, we're locked in. Do you believe it? This is the end of everything—Time-Savers, our reputations, everything. How will we live this down? Wait till Alan and Chris and everyone hear about this."

"Will you shut up?" he hissed. "They'll never hear about it. And Adrienne'll only leave us here longer if she thinks she's upset us. Just be quiet. Then it won't be any fun for her and she'll let us out."

So we waited. And waited. The shed was pitch-black. There was no window, and you couldn't see a thing. It wasn't any too warm either. Pete and I didn't speak. I hoped he'd learned some kind of lesson.

I don't know how long we sat in there, since of course I couldn't see my watch, but it felt like about an hour or so. We couldn't hear a sound. I was positive that by now the kids had let Persephone and Marco Polo out, that Joey was awake and crying, that Frankie and Cindy were playing with the stove, and that all the rest of the kids had been arrested for creating disturbances and had been carted down to the police station and would have to be claimed there by the Schwartzes. I wondered if baby-sitters still got paid when that happened.

At long last I heard another click in the doorknob. I jumped up. "Adrienne, you little—" Suddenly I froze in my tracks.

The door-opener was not Adrienne.

It was Mrs. Schwartz.

I gulped.

Pete jumped to his feet, too. He was standing so close to me I could feel his breath on my neck.

"Well, boys," began Mrs. Schwartz.

I hung my head and began to dream up the most apologetic story possible.

"I see Adrienne has played one of her little tricks on you. My niece has quite a sense of . . . of humor."

Pete and I stepped out of the shed and followed Mrs. Schwartz across the lawn and into the house.

"I hope you're not too upset," she went on.

I wasn't sure what to say, so I didn't say anything. Neither did Pete. I felt awfully uncomfortable. Especially when I heard a muffled "hee hee hee" close by.

"Maybe I should have warned you," Mrs. Schwartz continued. "Adrienne is . . . can be . . ."

At that point all I wanted was to leave. I cleared my throat. "Mrs. Schwartz—"

"Please," she interrupted. "All right. I know you're upset. But look, nothing happened. All the children are fine. They were playing safely indoors when we got home. I'm terribly sorry you were locked in the shed, but how about if I pay you each ten dollars? Will that make up for it?"

She stuffed a ten-dollar bill into each of our jacket pockets and hurried us toward the front door.

"Good-bye," she said as we stumbled onto the porch. "Thank you. I hope you'll come back and sit for us again soon."

"Fat chance," Pete mumbled.

" 'Bye, Mrs. Schwartz," I called loudly.

"Sit for her again? Is she crazy?" Pete exploded as soon as we were out of hearing range.

Pete had been very quiet ever since Adrienne locked us in. I guess he'd been building up steam all that time.

"Come on, Pete, it wasn't *so* bad. I mean, look—we earned *ten dollars* each."

"Yeah." He grinned at me.

We walked home slowly. It was growing dark. Front-porch lights and bedroom lights and living-room lights were being flicked on. We passed the Dodsons' house as Mrs. Dodson leaned out the door to whistle Nescafé in. Then we passed the Meiers' house as Mr. Meier came out and called for Cathy and Tommy. Nice evening sounds.

I forgot about being locked in the shed and thought about how I'd earned one-sixth of the Starcruiser.

We reached Pete's house.

" 'Night, Pete."

" 'Night, Mac."

The baby-sitting adventure was over.

10. Teaching James

"WEEE-OOOH."

Crash. Crash. Splinter.

James's Tinkertoy structure fell to the ground as he kicked and punched at its base.

"Weee-oooh, weee-oooh, weee-oooh."

James was good and mad. It was Wednesday evening. He'd been in school for three mornings, and the only result I could see was that he was angry all the time at home. He ran around the house, hands fluttering, weee-ooohing, and crying his no-tears cry. When we could get him to keep still long enough to build something, he'd build in a frenzy, fast and furious, with his hands trembling, and then he'd send his creation smashing to the floor.

A couple of times he'd punched himself. Last night when I tried to stop him, he bit my wrist and made it bleed. *Darn* him. So of course in school this morning, Alan asked what happened to my arm, and I forgot myself for a second and told the truth—my brother bit me—and now the whole class thinks I've got the weirdest brother in the world. They think James is crazy.

But what on earth was happening to James in his new school? What were the teachers doing to make him angry? It'd taken so long to get him into the Weston Child Development Institute, and for *this?*

Mom had been observing James at school—Dad, too, a couple of times—and she said he was very good there and that nothing awful happened to him. So I wanted to know what was going on. And I'd find out soon. In twenty minutes Dr. Wyman, the director of the WCDI, and Ms. Rinehart, James's speech teacher, were coming over.

I couldn't wait to meet them, but Lizzie was hiding out in her room. She was jealous. She said *her* teachers never took the trouble to come over for coffee and talk about *her* schoolwork. What was so special about James? I knew how she felt, but I did want to meet Dr. Wyman and Ms. Rinehart. Anything to make James calm down.

When the doorbell rang I was torn between wanting to answer it and wanting to go get Lizzie. But Dad answered the bell while Mom got hold of James, who'd gone dancing and weee-ooohing off toward the den. I went up to Lizzie's room and knocked on her door.

"They're here, Lizzie," I said.

"So what."

"Come on. You know you're supposed to come downstairs."

"No way."

"Liz-*zeee*. I thought you said you wanted to help teach James."

No answer.

"Lizzie? Will you let me in?"

"The door's open."

I walked in. Lizzie was sitting cross-legged on her bed, sorting through Dad's old baseball card collection. Her red cap was pulled down about as far as it would go.

"You said you'd teach, you know. We all did," I reminded her.

"Well, what do those two people have to do with anything?"

"They're James's teachers. They'll show us how they teach James so we can teach him the same way. Mom and Dad already explained that."

"What are you being such a big shot for, Jonno?" Lizzie's lower lip was trembling. "You were madder than anything at James for biting you."

"And I'm still mad. But aren't you even curious? I want to see what these people think they can teach him."

"Then go ahead."

That did it. I yanked Lizzie's baseball cap off her head and shouted, "Your hair stinks!" Then I slammed her door and stomped down the hall, feeling like a rat. But I wasn't going to apologize. If Lizzie wanted James to stay like he was, then she could suffer for it.

Downstairs Mom and Dad were serving coffee to a man and a woman seated on the couch.

Dad introduced us. "How do you do?" I said as I shook their hands.

They smiled at me. "Please call us Bill and Edie," said the director.

"And this is Lizzie," my father went on.

I whirled around, surprised to see her coming slowly down the stairs. Her eyes were a little red and her baseball cap was on crooked, but otherwise she looked O.K. She gave me a half smile, and I held up my pinkie finger, our secret signal meaning everything was all right.

"What we'd like to do this evening," said Bill, after we were all seated comfortably, "is simply talk with you a bit, observe James here in his home, and then show you some things you can work on with him."

"O.K.," said Dad.

Mom smiled.

"Where *is* James?" asked Lizzie.

He hadn't stayed around long after Mom caught him. He was never thrilled when we had visitors. Usually, he hid out in the den.

"I'll go get him," I said.

I walked into our den, which is at the back of the house, and switched on the ceiling light. There was James on the couch, sitting in the dark, for pete's sake.

"Geez, James," I said, totally exasperated. I took him by the hand and led him back to the living room.

"Weee-oooh, weee-oooh, weee-oooh." He howled all the way. As soon as he saw Bill and Edie, he looked particularly pained.

"Hey, I think he recognizes you!" I exclaimed.

I sat James by the collapsed Tinkertoy tower, hoping he'd start building. Otherwise, he'd leave again.

He gave a few whimpery weee-ooohs, then took the sticks I handed him and began to build listlessly. Bill watched him closely.

Nobody was talking, so I spoke up.

"I, um, have a question," I said, feeling a little scared. I hoped Bill and Edie wouldn't be offended when I asked it.

"Shoot, Jon," said Bill.

"Well," I began carefully, "ever since James started school on Monday, he's been... he's been sort of horrible at home." I held up my wrist as proof. "I thought school was going to *help* him."

"Oh, it is," said Bill, "at least, we think so. Nothing is ever a sure bet. But what James is going through now is pretty normal. It's a reaction."

"A reaction?" I asked. "Like an allergic reaction?"

"In a way," said Edie. "See, we're putting a lot of pressure on James in school. We're making demands on him. We're asking him to do things he's never had to do before, like hang up his jacket, wash his hands, put away his toys. He's used to having those things done for him. Since he's not sure about us or the school, and doesn't know how we'll react if he gets mad, he's doing all his getting mad at home. It's hard for children like James to trust people, so he's not taking any chances with the new faces at school. But he trusts you a little more and probably thinks it's O.K. to get mad around you."

"Oh," I said slowly, thinking this over. "Will he stop?"

"He will," said Bill, "if you'll help him."

I glanced at Lizzie. She knew I was looking at her, but she wouldn't look back.

"How do we help?" asked Dad. "What do we do?"

"Well, this is something I wanted to talk to you about tonight," said Bill.

Then Mom and Dad and Bill and Edie started talking. They talked for almost forty-five minutes. I listened carefully and tried to follow everything they were saying but I got lost quite a few times. The main thing I understood was that we were supposed to reward James for doing things we wanted him to do, and punish him for doing things we didn't want him to do. The rewards would be feeding him Cheerios, or saying "Good boy, James!" with a big smile, or hugging him (if he'd let us). The punishments would be not giving him Cheerios, or saying "No, James," without any smile.

At first I thought it sounded pretty easy, but it turned out you had to do this all the time—for practically *everything*. We were supposed to do it at meals to get him to try new foods and not barf. We were supposed to sit him on the toilet a few times a day and reward him if he happened to go. We were supposed to reward him for building nicely or coming to us for a hug or trying to put his clothes on, and we were supposed to punish him for weee-ooohing or punching himself or biting me or fluttering his hands.

My head was a total jumble, but Edie said, "It's not as hard as it sounds. I'll demonstrate something to you. Have you noticed how hard it is to get James to look you in the eye?"

We all nodded. It was almost impossible. He'd look anywhere but in your eyes.

"Well," said Edie, "this is typical of autistic children. It's scary for them. It means they have to come out of their own world and open themselves up to other people. Looking someone in the eye is a sign of trust or intimacy, and James doesn't want that." She glanced at Lizzie to see if Lizzie was following her, which was very nice. I liked Edie and Bill more and more.

"What I mean," Edie continued, seeing Lizzie's frustrated face, "is that most autistic children feel threatened by making eye contact. But that's the first thing we teach them. It's important because when a child is making eye contact we know he or she is paying attention. I'll show you. Could I have some Cheerios for James?"

"Sure," said Lizzie, wondering what was going to happen. It was kind of like a magic show.

In a few minutes, Lizzie came out of the kitchen with a dish of Cheerios.

James zeroed in on them immediately, but Lizzie was pretty quick and handed them right to Edie. James stood in the middle of the room with his eyes on those Cheerios.

Edie held the dish out to him. "James?" she asked. "Do you want Cheerios?"

James took a step closer.

"Do you want Cheerios?" Edie asked again.

James walked all the way over to Edie and stood next to

her, never taking his eyes off the cereal.

Edie took a few Cheerios out of the dish and held them up by her face. "James, look at me," she said.

James looked a little confused. He wanted those Cheerios *so* badly.

"James, look at me."

James's eyes flickered to Edie's for just a fraction of a second. I think it was just by accident.

"Good boy!" Edie cried as she popped some Cheerios in his mouth and gave him a hug.

Immediately she tried it again, holding the Cheerios up to her face. "James, look at me."

"Weee-oooh!" shrieked James, and flapped out of the room, crunching a couple of Tinkertoy pieces on the way.

In a flash, Bill was after him. He picked James up in one swift movement, carried him back into the living room, and plopped him on the couch next to Edie.

Edie tried again, but James gazed stubbornly off into space. Boy, was he surprised when Edie hid the cereal behind her back and said sternly, "No, James."

Before he could get too upset, Edie put the dish back in her lap and started working again. James looked at her once more.

"Wow!" I couldn't help shouting after the last time. "James learned something! He really did!"

"Why don't you try it now?" suggested Bill. "James has to learn to look at other people besides Edie. We have to be sure he knows what 'look at me' means."

"*Me* try it?" I asked.

"Sure," said Edie. She leaned over and gave me the Cheerios.

"Should I sit on the couch like you?"

"No, stay there. Let's make the game a little different and see if James understands."

"O.K.," I said nervously. I was sitting on the floor by the Tinkertoys. "James?" I asked, just like Edie had done. "Do you want Cheerios?"

He sure did. He might not have wanted to look at me, but he wanted his Cheerios all right.

He walked right over to me and stood in front of me. I left the cereal on the floor and said, "James, look at me." He waited a few seconds, then glanced uncertainly at me. I gave him some Cheerios and a gigantic hug. James, you really can learn, I thought. If only the in-kids could see this. They wouldn't think you're crazy.

After that, everyone including Lizzie, tried the look-at-me game, but James had had enough. Or maybe he was full of Cheerios. Anyway, he wouldn't look at anyone else. Edie said progress would be slow. Still, James had looked at Edie and me, even if it was just for a second, so I knew one thing for sure. We *could* teach James. He was going to be O.K. after all.

It wasn't until I was in bed that night and almost asleep that I remembered Noodle. Noodle was Termite's sisters' dachshund. He was at college with one of the sisters now, but what I remembered was two summers ago when Pete and Termite and I taught Noodle to beg and roll over. We did it exactly the way Edie and Bill were teaching James to look-at-me. One of us would hold a dog biscuit out to Noodle and say, "Roll over, Noodle." If he did it right, he got the biscuit. If he didn't, no biscuit, and maybe a little scolding.

Great. Was James becoming a trained dog, just like Noodle? Look at me, James, and you'll get your Cheerios. Hang up your jacket and you'll get a reward. Here, James, here, boy. Good James, good dog.

It was a long time before I fell asleep that night. I had a lot to think about.

11. My Brilliant Idea

March is supposed to come in like a lion and go out like a lamb. But this March was backward. It had come in like a lamb with warm, sunny weather the first week or so, then had become more and more lionish, with cold air and gray days and a few little snowstorms. And on the night of March 31 we had an honest-to-goodness blizzard, which meant April came in like a lion.

Now it was the middle of April, and after all the blizzards and stuff, spring was finally here. I wondered if James noticed. I knew spring was not a terribly cool thing to think about; I was sure Alan and Chris and the others didn't care about chirping birdies or blooming flowers, but I did. And I had an idea Pete and Termite and Stephanie and Claudia did, too. Or maybe everyone did and the difference between the in-kids and the rest of us was that we would admit it and they wouldn't. It was hard to tell.

This is what I was thinking over one warm April afternoon as I sat on our front porch after school. I wasn't exactly bored, but I couldn't think of anything to do, either. So I sat and dreamed.

After a little while a blue VW van pulled up our driveway. The driver got out, jogged around to the back door, and opened it. Slowly, very slowly, James eased himself and his Flintstones lunchbox off the seat and down the step. The step was pretty high, but the driver let James alone, and James managed everything fine.

He'd been going to school full days for a week now. He didn't get home until three-thirty or four in the afternoon. It seemed like a long day for a four-year-old. On the other hand, James wasn't any ordinary four-year-old.

The driver slammed the door shut and said good-bye to James. James flapped his free hand in front of his eyes and galloped over to me.

"Hi, James," I said with a smile.

"Oh-*ma*," he answered.

I sighed.

A piece of white paper was pinned to James's jacket. It didn't say who it was for, so I unfastened it and read it.

> Dear Petersons,
> Please send in separate photographs of every member of your family. If possible, they should be fairly recent so James can recognize them. I need them for speech sessions. Thanks!
>
> Edie

That was strange. Edie and the other teachers had done a few unusual things with James, like encouraging him to roll around on a mat so he could start learning to laugh and play, but what was she going to do with photographs?

I took James and the note in the house. I wondered if this was important enough to interrupt Mom for. She was working in her study. Now that James was settled in school, she and

Dad observed there only a couple of hours every week, which meant Mom had a lot more time for copywriting. She'd taken on more projects in the last month than she had in the past two years. I was afraid all the work might make her tired, but she seemed really happy instead.

James and I were hesitating at the study door just as Mom opened it and came out.

"Well, hello, you two!" she exclaimed. "James, you're home." She kissed his cheek. "How was school?"

He didn't answer, of course, but Edie had said it was important to talk to him like he was a regular kid.

"Mom, look at this note from Edie." I held it out.

Mom scanned it. "That's funny. I wonder...oh, well. James, come on and we'll find the pictures for Edie." She led him off toward the den and the family photograph albums.

I wandered back out to the porch. After a while Termite came over.

"Hey!" I greeted him.

"Hey," he answered. "I saw James come home. How's he doing?"

"Pretty well. He ate a whole serving of peas last night because Dad gave him a Cheerio after every bite. He didn't even barf. And sometimes he repeats words if you tell him to. He can say *hi* and *'bye*."

"That's really great, Mac," said Termite, but he didn't sound all that impressed.

"Had any Time-Savers calls?" I asked after a while.

"The last one was two weeks ago. How about you?"

"Mr. Phomalont called yesterday. He needs their first-floor windows washed. Other than him, no one's called in about a week and a half."

"Business is slacking off," said Termite dejectedly.

"Yeah. I've only earned twenty-seven dollars and nineteen cents toward the Starcruiser. I've got a long way to go."

"We better do something."

"Like what?"

"Like get Pete. He'll know what to do!"

We ran over to Pete's house, hoping he didn't have any homework so he could come out.

Pete, it turned out, didn't have any homework left, but he didn't want to come out either, so we went up to his room.

"We have to have a conference," I said as we sprawled out on his floor. "A business conference."

"Right," said Termite. "Time-Savers is failing."

"What?" shouted Pete.

"Well, when was the last time you got a call?" I asked him. Pete was silent, thinking.

"That long, huh?" said Termite.

"Just a second, just a second . . ."

"Never mind, Pete. We get a call every now and then, but not like before," I said. "People are forgetting about us."

"Yeah, they've probably lost our fliers." Termite toyed with Pete's printing press.

"That's it!" cried Pete. The old idea glint was in his eyes. I'd been hoping to see that glint. "It's simple. What we have to do is *revamp* Time-Savers!"

Termite and I glanced at each other. "Do what?" asked Termite.

"Revamp it," repeated Pete. "You know, spruce it up."

"Yeah," I said. "We could make up a new flier. Hey, maybe even put an ad in the newspaper!"

"Yeah!" Pete and Termite shouted. "Who gets the paper?"

"We do," I said. "It should be delivered any minute now. That is . . ."

"What?"

"Oh, just that it hasn't come the last two days for some reason, but let's go wait anyway."

We charged back over to my porch.

"I think I'll give Lizzie another chance to be part of the business," I said while we waited. "She should be home soon."

"Where is she?" asked Termite.

"At a Brownie meeting."

"At a Brownie meeting! What's she doing going to Brownies? She's never done anything like that before. Sheesh," exclaimed Termite.

"She just joined a few weeks ago. She really seems to like it. She hardly ever hangs around with Wendell anymore."

At that moment Lizzie ran up the front lawn in her brown dress and brown sweater and brown socks and brown shoes and red baseball cap. A little brown beanie was supposed to be part of the uniform, but Lizzie refused to wear it. She said she preferred her cap. It did more for her hair. Her troop leader called my mother one evening to find out about the cap, and after Mom explained, Lizzie was allowed to wear it to meetings, as long as she promised to wear the brown beanie in the Memorial Day Parade.

"Lizzie," I said, "we're . . . we're *revamping* Time-Savers. Do you want to be part of it now? We could put your name on the new fliers."

"Thanks, Jonno, but I've got other things to do. I have to go now."

"Where are you going?"

"Up to my room. And don't come in unless you knock first. 'Bye, Pete, 'bye, Termite."

She dashed off.

"Lizzie has sure been spending a lot of time in her room lately," commented Pete.

"I know," I said. "I wish I knew what she was up to."

"Maybe it's so she can hide out from James," said Termite.

He would think that.

"Geez, Termite," said Pete, which was just what I wanted to say.

There was an embarrassing silence.

"Well," I said, "anyway, James is much better."

And as if to prove it, Mom and James came out to take a walk.

"See?" I said as they moved slowly down the driveway. "James's hands aren't fluttering as much. He only said weee-oooh a few times this morning. And he's almost looking straight ahead."

I knew it didn't sound like much.

"For heaven's sake, where's the paper?" burst out Pete.

"I don't know. This is the third day in a row it hasn't been delivered. Last night Mom had to go out and buy it. . . . *Hey!*"

"What?" cried Pete and Termite.

"I just thought of something. I've got to go make a phone call. This could be really important!"

12. The Newspaper Disaster

Three days later I rolled out of bed at five A.M. I looked outside. Still dark. I got dressed as quietly as I could, ran downstairs, and hopped on my bike. It was kind of exciting.

I rode through the shadowy, silent streets, looking at the dark windows of the houses and thinking about all the people asleep inside.

It was the first morning of my paper route. What I'd found out from my phone call was that our paper hadn't been delivered for three days because our paperboy had quit without even telling anybody. And sure enough, they needed somebody to take over his route. I'd felt pretty proud of myself after I made the call. I mean, I'd felt really nervous on the phone, but I'd just tried to be polite and calm. When someone answered the phone at the newspaper office, I'd said, "Hello, my name is Jonathan Peterson. I live on Napanee Road, and our paper hasn't been delivered for three days."

"Yes," said the woman on the other end, "we're sorry. We're not charging you for it, but the newsboy who usually takes your route has...left...."

That was my chance. I hoped I wouldn't blow it. "I—you're

not—are you looking for anybody to take over his route?" I managed to ask.

"Well, as a matter of fact . . . Do you know of anyone who might be interested?"

"Yes, ma'am," I said, trying to sound enthusiastic and polite and responsible and grown up. "I do. I'd be interested."

"How old are you?" she asked.

"Eleven," I said. "Almost twelve." (I only had five-and-a-half months to go.)

"Could you come to our office tomorrow so we can meet you?"

"Sure," I said. If Mom couldn't drive me, I'd ride my bike.

"Fine," she said. "Four o'clock?"

"Four o'clock," I repeated. "I'll see you tomorrow."

She told me her name and we hung up.

When I got off the phone, I was so excited I let out a whoop and went cheering and jumping outside to tell Pete and Termite.

The next day, Mom drove me to the newspaper office. She said she might have to sign papers or something, you never know. But she didn't come in with me. I wouldn't let her. I made her stay in the car. For one thing, James was with her, and I wanted to make a good impression. Which would be hard to do if James weee-ooohed or hit himself or started yelling and fluttering.

The interview was really easy. I talked to two people, and they just wanted to know what school I went to and what grade I was in. Stuff like that. Then they told me what I'd have to do to keep up the paper route, and asked me if I honestly thought I could handle it. They reminded me about how the last boy had quit. The job didn't sound easy, that was for sure, but I said I thought I could do it. It paid pretty well.

So the next afternoon, I followed this girl, Maureen, around on her paper route to make sure I knew the procedure, and this morning I was on my own. The *Tribune* came out every weekday afternoon and on Tuesday, Friday, and Sunday mornings—the Coupon Clippers Club Morning Special.

I reached the corner of Random Road and Swing Lane as the sky was beginning to lighten a little. Nobody was on the corner. I parked my bike and stood there, fingering the canvas *Tribune* sack that was tied around my middle.

After about five minutes, Maureen rode up. "Hi!" she called, swinging expertly off her bike before it even stopped. She parked it next to mine.

"Hi," I answered.

"You all ready?" she asked.

"I guess so," I said. "All I really have to learn is who's on the route so I don't have to look at the addresses so much." I took the plastic-covered piece of paper with my route listed on it out of the *Tribune* bag and studied it.

"You'll know the whole thing by heart in four or five days," said Maureen. "You'll be surprised."

"The other thing I'm not sure about is collecting the money. I wonder what morning I should do that."

Maureen started laughing.

"What's so funny?" I asked.

"Are you kidding?" she spluttered, trying to get back in control. "You can't collect the money in the morning. Your customers would kill you." She looked at her watch. "It's five thirty, for pete's sake. You have to collect after school."

I blushed furiously. "Oh. Right."

Luckily, the newspaper van drove up just then, and three more kids arrived, two on bikes, one with a wagon. A man wearing a brown *Tribune* uniform swung himself out of the front and slid open the doors on the side. "Morning, everybody," he shouted cheerfully.

"Good morning, Max," the rest of the kids called back.

Max started to unload stacks of papers.

Two more boys arrived.

"What do we have here?" asked Max as he dumped a pile of papers in front of me. "Oh, you're the new kid, right?"

I nodded.

"Well, good luck." He grinned at me.

"Thanks," I said. I counted out thirty Coupon Clippers Club Morning Specials, one for everybody on my route, and began stuffing them in my bag. I had this feeling all the kids were watching me. I hate being the new anything. I hoped I was doing everything right. Was I supposed to be folding the papers or something? Was everyone watching me be a total foul-up?

Finally I glanced up. Most of the kids were getting ready to ride off. Max had gotten back in the truck and was starting the motor. He flashed me the thumbs-up sign. I waved to him. Nobody said anything to me, so I jumped on my bike and pedaled toward Vandeventer.

My route was not a really long one, which was O.K. with me. It meant I didn't get paid quite as much, of course, since you get paid according to how many papers you deliver, but I decided it was just as well to have a short route at first. There was an awful lot to remember. The people on my route were on Vandeventer, a short street that intersected with mine; Poe Road, another short street; and Napanee.

I decided to start with Vandeventer. I rode to the corner, checked my chart to see the first address on the route, and walked my bike to the driveway. Then I folded the paper the way Maureen had shown me the day before, and threw it, aiming for the front porch. It landed smack on the doormat. I smiled to myself and coasted down the sidewalk to the next address. Again I folded the paper and tossed it. Another bull's-eye.

I was feeling pretty proud of myself by the time I reached the third house. I couldn't see the front porch too well because there were all these overgrown bushes around it, but I aimed and tossed the paper anyway.

Thud.

"Grrrowooooof!"

This gigantic dog tore off the front porch. I must have hit him. He gallumphed right at me, barking and snarling. A window shade snapped up in a second-floor window, but I didn't stick around to see what would happen. I just jumped on my bicycle and lit down the street as fast as my legs could pump.

I overshot the next house on the route, but I didn't care. The important thing was to lose that incredible hulk of a dog. Finally I put on the brakes and turned to look behind me. Superdog was sauntering home. He had this air about him that said, "I guess I showed *him.*" He looked suave and cool, like one of the in-boys after he's been teasing Edweird.

I stopped my bike, turned around, and went back to the house I'd missed. The front porch was all clear. I tossed the paper.

It landed on the roof.

I guess my shooting was a little off after the last experience. What the heck was I supposed to do *now?*

I had exactly twenty-six Coupon Clippers Specials left, and exactly twenty-six more houses to deliver them to. One of the houses was my own. I wondered if Mom and Dad could do without their coupons for one morning. But that wouldn't make me look so hot.

I sighed and got off my bicycle. Then I stood on the sidewalk, scratching my head. Who's house was this, anyway? I wondered. I got out the list of addresses. 42 Vandeventer. Giancossi.

Oh, no, I groaned, smacking the palm of my hand to my forehead. Of all houses, this was *Chris Giancossi's.*

Oh, no, I groaned again.

I looked at my watch. Almost six. I'd promised Mom I'd be back by six forty-five every morning. On the dot.

So.

I could forget about the Giancossis' paper, or give them ours, or try to figure out some way to get the paper off the roof. Three choices. None of them very inspiring.

I looked the house over. One part of it was one story high; another part was two stories high. The paper had landed near the edge of the lower roof just above the front door and right under a bedroom window on the second story. The Giancossis' backyard was closed in by a stockade fence. I think they had a pool back there.

I was still standing by my bike, thinking. The papers were getting pretty heavy, so I put them down.

Then I checked out that fence again. It looked like it went right up to the edge of the roof in back of the house. Maybe if I could climb up the fence, I could get on the roof, crawl over the top, and drop the paper down onto the porch. Actually, it wouldn't be hard to do, but I sure didn't want anyone to see me. And it was pretty light out by now. You could probably get arrested for what I was doing. What was it—trespassing? Sneaking around? Unlawful paper removal? On the other hand, I was just doing my job.

I propped my bike against a phone pole and left it leaning there with the nearly full *Tribune* bag next to it. Watch, everything would probably be stolen before I got back.

I looked up and down the street, saw that no cars were coming, and made sure the Giancossis' window shades were drawn on the second floor. Then I dashed around the side of the house.

After looking over the fence for a few seconds, I grabbed the top of one stockade, or whatever all those wooden things are called, slapped my sneakers up against the fence, and did a pretty good Spiderman imitation right up the side. When I reached the top, I was all bunched up, hands and feet together. I looked like Pete's old cat, Kiki, who used to sleep with his feet and his tail slung together in one pile near his head.

I grabbed for the edge of the roof, lost my balance, teetered, and righted myself just in time. A good thing, too. The Giancossis would have been pretty surprised to find a body by their stockade fence when they woke up that morning.

Shaking a little from the near miss, I clutched the gutter and crawled onto the roof. Luckily, the gutter held.

SKRITCH.

I moved my left knee forward.

SKRITCH.

I moved my left hand forward.

SKRITCH.

Every move I made sounded like a whole army of newspaper thieves on the Giancossis' roof.

Oh, well. I couldn't do a thing about it.

I crawled to the peak, by the wall of the higher roof. At least I wasn't so out in the open. I looked over the roof and checked on my bike and newspapers. Still there.

Gingerly, leaning against the wall for support, I eased myself over the peak.

SKREEETCH.

Suddenly I started sliding and didn't stop till I was halfway down the other side of the roof. Somebody must have heard it. I was right under that bedroom window. I lay still, trying to make myself very small.

I didn't hear a sound.

I took a huge breath.

The newspaper was about six inches away from my right foot. I sat up, slid forward, and kicked the paper over the edge.

I had made it. Almost.

Just then a head poked out of the window. It was Chris.

"Nice work, Peterson," he called.

Oh, no.

I would never ever ever live this down. But I didn't want to appear too upset. "Thanks!" I called.

I began the climb back to the fence.

Five minutes later I was dusting myself off and then jogging around to the front yard.

I hopped on my bike and rode off to deliver the rest of the Coupon Clippers Club Morning Specials, but all the excitement was gone from the job. Chris wouldn't let something like this go by. I knew I'd hear about it in school.

Boy, would I hear about it.

13. Getting Better

A couple of hours after that wonderful newspaper experience, I was sitting in our classroom with Pete and Termite. Mr. Westoff had recently arranged our desks in groups of four. Our group was Pete and me and Claudia and Stephanie.

I watched the kids trickle in.

Edweird arrived earlier than usual. He was wearing white shoes and baggy tan pants that were held up with suspenders, if you can believe it. Brother. I was almost glad. I was anticipating a little trouble from Chris, but I figured Edweird's outfit would be good competition for the razzing.

Edweird flumped onto a chair, huffing and all out of breath. He must have been running or something. Edweird hardly ever participates in gym. Our teacher lets him sit on the bench a lot.

Pete nudged me and pointed at Edweird. He had just caught sight of the white shoes and suspenders.

"I know," I said. "Too weird. Too-weird Edweird."

Pete grinned.

Edweird's huffing was slowing down. He looked around the room and caught us staring at him. "Hi, Jonathan!" he

called. "Hi, Peter! Hi..." He didn't know Termite's name.
"Hi, there!"

"Hi," we mumbled.

Then Edweird did something new. He heaved himself out of his seat and lumbered over to us.

"Oh, *no*," whispered Termite, sounding panicky the way he does when he sees James get out of control. "What's he doing?"

I rolled my eyes. "I don't know."

"Aw, geez," said Pete under his breath. "Aw, geez."

Edweird was standing by our group. He struggled to sit on one of the desks, like we were doing. It took him a few tries. He kept slipping back.

I hoped really hard that I'd never get as fat as Edweird.

"Good morning, boys," Edweird said, when he finally managed to get his bulk arranged on Stephanie's desk. "How are you today?"

Why did Edweird sound as if he'd learned to speak from one of those foreign-language records?

"Fine, Edwei—Edward," I muttered.

Chris and Hank came in just at that moment. They *would*. They didn't even try to hide their laughter.

Hee, hee, hee. Very funny.

They stood in a corner snorting and snickering and pointing at us.

Termite had had enough. "See ya," he said disgustedly, and marched out of the room.

I watched him. It was worth it. As he got out the door, he turned so he was facing Chris's and Hank's backs. He twisted his mouth and rolled his eyes so his pupils were up inside his head and all you could see were the whites. Then he pointed at Chris and Hank, bobbing his head and letting his tongue hang out. He waited until he knew he had Pete and me smiling before he ran down the hall.

Elise and Janie came in.

"Hello," they said sweetly to Chris and Hank.

"Hi," said the boys. "Hey, come here."

"What?"

The boys pulled them into the corner and started whispering and snickering and pointing at us again. Janie and Elise began giggling.

I hate it when they giggle. They sound so fake.

"How are your parents?" asked Edweird suddenly.

Pete and I didn't even bother to answer.

"I hope they're well."

"Come on," I said. Pete and I hopped off the desks and headed for the coat closet. If Edweird followed, it would take him a few minutes to catch up.

"Hey, Jon," yelled Chris from the front of the room, "how's your paper route?"

I scowled.

"Are you deaf?" shouted Hank. He raised his voice as much as he could without letting the vice-principal overhear us. "CHRIS ASKED YOU HOW YOUR PAPER ROUTE IS."

"FINE," I hollered back.

"*I'm* not deaf," said Hank maddeningly. "You don't have to yell at *me.*"

"Then why are you—" I started to shout back, but Pete put his hand on my shoulder. "Cool out," he muttered. "Forget it."

"Hey, Jon," called Chris again. "Do you deliver all your papers on the roof, or is that just a special favor for us?"

"It was no favor," I said loudly. "I don't do favors for jerks."

The class fell silent, sensing trouble. The bell was about to ring, and almost everyone had arrived. Except Mr. Westoff, of course.

"Jon—" Claudia started to say.

She was standing next to me, but I wasn't looking at her. My eyes were glued to Chris. He looked like a bull getting ready to charge. You could practically see smoke coming out of his ears. I'd never been in a fight at school (or anywhere else, for that matter). It looked like now was going to be my first time.

I tensed up, getting ready to defend myself if Chris charged. But he didn't charge. Suddenly his whole face changed— softened, sort of. I still didn't trust him, though.

He positioned himself in the middle of the classroom and said, "I saw that dopey little brother of Jon's riding on the retarded bus yesterday."

The class snickered appreciatively.

"I think you're the dopey one, Chris," Stephanie said, which surprised me because usually she's pretty quiet. "Buses can't be retarded."

The class snickered again. Even Elise and the other in-girls laughed.

I flashed Steph a grateful smile.

"No," said Chris uncomfortably, "but Jon's brother can be. Man, is he weird. A real retardo." Chris started fluttering his hands around.

More laughter.

"And," he went on, "he's not the only weird one." He glared meaningfully at Edweird, who flushed and then stumbled, trying to get off Steph's desk.

Part of me wanted to crawl into a hole and hide there forever. Another part of me wanted to give Chris and the others just what they deserved. I started forming words in my head and opened my mouth to let the in-boys have it—for once, just for *once*—when Mr. Westoff hurried into the room.

Immediately everyone scattered, clambering for their desks. Saved again.

That night, after the newspaper disaster and the rotten morning at school, I was really beat. All I could think of was going to bed. The sooner the better. But at dinner, Mom reminded everybody that Bill and Edie were coming over. I had to stay up for that. It was important.

When dinner was over, Mom and Dad cleaned up the kitchen while Lizzie got to watch TV and I had to read James his story. How come I always got stuck with him? I sat him on the living-room couch next to me and opened up this baby book called *Pat the Bunny*. James sat quietly for about three seconds. Then he jumped up suddenly and exclaimed, "Oh-ma!"

"Come on, James," I said tiredly, pulling him back down on the couch.

"Weee-oooh!" he cried. He leaped up again.

Maybe he didn't like the book. Or maybe he had a stomachache. Or maybe he suddenly remembered something bad that happened two or three years ago. How could you tell *any*thing with James?

"Ja-ames," I scolded. I sat him down roughly. I was too tired to fool around with whatever his problem was.

"Weee-oooh, weee-oooh, weee-oooh," he whined nervously.

He started to flap his hands. I knew he wasn't supposed to do it.

"No, James," I said sharply.

He flapped harder.

"No, James." I slapped his hand and turned my back on him. When I turned around to look at him a few seconds later, his hands were almost still. Wow, that worked pretty well, I told myself. "Good boy, James!" I praised him.

Pat the Bunny had fallen on the floor. I picked it up and started in on page three.

Without warning, James snatched the book out of my hands, bending the cover. "Weeeeee!" he shrieked. He was trembling with rage.

"Mom!" I called. "Dad!"

Dad ran into the living room.

James had careened off the couch and was standing on the floor, stamping his feet and hitting his face.

"You handle him," I said crossly to Dad, and marched into the den to watch TV with Lizzie.

After a few minutes, though, I began to feel guilty. Just as I was about to head back into the living room to apologize, the doorbell rang. I ran to answer it, but Dad beat me to it.

As Bill and Edie were hanging up their coats, I said to Dad, "I'm really sorry." I'd have spent the whole evening worrying if I hadn't apologized.

"That's O.K., son," he said quietly. "You were angry." He patted me on the back.

I smiled up at him.

"Problems?" asked Bill.

"James is a little upset," said Dad as we found chairs in the living room. "Jonno's been handling him very well, but he's had a hard day today."

In the back of the house I could hear Mom calling Lizzie. Then she came into the living room with James. Dad must have handed him over to her.

James skirted tensely around Bill and Edie. He almost danced right back out of the room, but Lizzie caught him on her way in.

"Come on," she said. She sat on the floor and pulled James into her lap, where he squirmed and struggled.

"Well," said Edie. "How are things?"

Everyone began talking at once.

We laughed and started over.

After a few minutes, Edie said, "James, come here."

James stayed put until Lizzie heaved him upright and pushed him toward Edie.

On the way his eyes darted to hers briefly. It looked like an accident, but Edie exclaimed, "Good boy!" and gave him a hug.

James accepted it stiffly.

Edie checked the table next to her and saw that a bowl of Cheerios had been placed on it.

It was funny. We did that automatically now before Bill and Edie came over, the way you'd put out nuts or potato chips before a cocktail party.

Edie took a few Cheerios. "Hi, James," she said clearly.

"Ha!" he answered.

"Good boy!" Edie gave him Cheerios and a smile. Then she pulled an envelope out of her purse. From the envelope she took five photographs. They were the photos of our family that Mom had found for James the other day.

"This is really something," said Edie to all of us. "James has been working very hard on it. His progress is slow, but still, it's progress.... Come here, big guy," she said as she hoisted James up on the couch and sat him so he was facing her. Then she spread out three of the photos—Mom, me, and Lizzie. "James," Edie said, to get his attention.

He appeared not to hear her.

"James," she said again.

He looked at her reluctantly.

"Touch Mommy," said Edie.

James looked down at the pictures and considered. "Weee-oooh," he moaned. Finally he stuck his finger out hesitantly in the direction of the picture of Mom.

"Oh, *good* boy!" cried Edie. She rewarded him quickly, before he could make a mistake or get upset.

"Wow!" I shouted.

"Yeah," said Lizzie.

Mom and Dad were grinning.

Edie mixed up the five photos and laid down a different group. "James, touch Lizzie," she said.

But James squirmed off the couch like a frightened rabbit. Edie let him go. "That's enough for now," she said. "He's been working hard. This is difficult and a little scary for him."

I could feel this seed of excitement growing in my stomach. James was going to get well. I just knew it. Even if we did have to train him like a circus dog. He was smart after all.

I left the room to find James, and when I brought him back, Dad took him upstairs to bed. I was getting more tired by the minute, but I stuck around to hear whatever else Bill and Edie might have to say.

We talked about James for a bit, and then Bill mentioned that the Weston Child Development Institute was having a fund-raiser the next weekend.

"What's a fund-raiser?" asked Lizzie.

"It's a project to raise money for something," said Bill. "WCDI is very expensive to run, and we need money for new equipment. So next Saturday, if you come to Palmer Square in Weston, you'll find tables set up and people selling brownies and cakes and cookies and handmade things. The money we earn will go toward some playground toys and teaching materials for James and the other kids."

"Yum," said Lizzie dreamily. "Brownies..."

"Could we help out?" asked Mom. "We make mean fudge around here."

"We need all the help we can get," said Edie earnestly. "The chairman of the fund-raising committee should be calling you any day now. It sometimes takes him a while to contact the families of new students, but once he does, the whole family is usually involved."

Dad came back downstairs and sat down near Mom.

"Can I ask something?" I said.

"Always." Bill smiled.

"Well, I was just thinking. We pay...we pay...tuition, right? To send James to WCDI? The other kids must, too. So how come you need more money? What's James's tuition for?"

"Good question," said Bill. "It's for lots of things—the teachers' salaries, equipment, food, renting the rooms we use for the school. The state *gives* all that money to towns to run public schools, but special schools like WCDI don't usually get much help from the government. So we have to depend on the families of the students. And some of them don't have much money at all. Then we let them pay less money. We'd hate to turn a child away from school just because the family was having trouble making ends meet. But then *we* don't have enough money to run the school."

"Oh," I said. "I see." It was complicated. Was it fair that we paid more tuition than some families? And what if Bill and Edie couldn't raise enough money to keep WCDI going? What would happen to James?

I decided not to worry, though. I decided to think about James getting better.

* * *

Later that night, after Bill and Edie had left and Lizzie had gone to sleep, and I was falling asleep myself even though I was still down in the living room with Mom and Dad, I said groggily, "Old James is pretty neat."

"Neat," repeated Dad, with a smile. "I guess he is at that, Jonno."

"I'm really proud of him," I said. "He recognized your picture, Mom."

"We're proud, too." Mom grinned.

"He's going to get well now, isn't he?" I said. I was hardly expecting an answer; I was so sure Mom and Dad would be thinking the same thing.

They glanced at each other.

"Jonno," said Mom slowly, "with James, you take things one step at a time and just see how they go. You don't predict or plan where he's concerned."

"But he's *talk*ing, Mom."

"Honey, he's beginning to learn a couple of words, which he uses only when you ask him a question or when you tell him to say one of them. . . . Do you know how big your vocabulary was when you were almost five?"

"No."

"It must have been hundreds of words. It was so big, Daddy and I had stopped counting when you were three. You talked a blue streak. So did Lizzie; so do most other almost-five-year-olds."

I stared uncomfortably at the floor.

"You talked about cars and trucks and books and TV shows. You made up long stories and told them to Lizzie. You sang songs and memorized commercials and—"

"All right, all right," I said.

"Jonno, we're pleased with James's progress," Dad put in.

"It's just that it's *so* slow. We thought school would make more of a difference with James—that he'd change faster."

I nodded.

"But Edie and Bill have told us several times to be patient. They said progress is sometimes painfully slow," added Dad.

"They did?" I asked.

"Yes," said Dad. "I guess we just wanted to believe that somehow James wouldn't be like other autistic children. He'd be an exception. We want...so much for him."

I nodded again. I knew what he meant. "But," I added, "James is really trying, I think. He's trying as hard as he can."

"Yes," said Mom. "I think he is trying."

Dad didn't say anything.

14. Spring Vacation

Vacation at last! There's nothing I like better than vacation—day after day of sleeping late, and catching all the TV shows you miss when you're in school, and no homework, and endless time to do whatever you want.

It was Easter vacation, only the school called it spring vacation. We had a weekend, a whole week, and another weekend off. Nine straight days of freedom, including three special events. One was Easter, which would fall on the first Sunday of the vacation; one was James's birthday, which we were going to celebrate the following Saturday, even though his birthday was on Thursday; and one wasn't very exciting but was pretty interesting—Lizzie and I were going to visit James at his school for the first time. (James didn't get a spring vacation.)

On Easter morning I had to get up at five A.M. to deliver the paper. It had to be delivered even on Easter Sunday. I was pretty good with the paper now. I could fold it up really fast, and when I threw it, it almost always landed on the front porch. Except for that one house—the one where Superdog lived. Usually I left Superdog's paper somewhere in the middle of his front lawn. So far, his owners hadn't complained.

I had collection worked out, too. I collected every other Tuesday afternoon. If any of my customers weren't home that day, I'd check back the next afternoon and the next and the next until I found them at home. My customers were all good about paying, and it was beginning to look like that Starcruiser could be mine after all.

In fact, it looked so possible that now I wasn't sure whether I wanted the $62.99 Starcruiser, or this $85.98 automatic baseball pitcher that was also at Kaler's. Pete had pointed out that if I bought the baseball pitcher, we could open up a baseball training institute in my backyard this summer and earn money training the neighborhood kids for Little League. He said that in no time at all I'd earn back the money spent on the pitcher, and then I could buy the Starcruiser, too. I said I'd have to think it over.

Easter morning I got home right at the dot of six forty-five and delivered my thirtieth paper to the kitchen table. Everyone was still asleep. I headed upstairs, thinking I might catch a few more Z's myself, but I heard an odd thumping sound coming from James's room, so I unlocked his door to check on him. (We latch his door at night because once he started getting up really early in the morning, like around three or four, and wandering through the house weee-ooohing. We were afraid he'd hurt himself or accidentally catch the house on fire or something.)

I eased his door open. James was standing by his bed. He was staring at me. Not into my eyes, just at my body.

"James?" I asked softly. I was trying to figure out what the thumping sound had been.

He continued staring at me. It was as if he could see right through me. I shivered. James scares me sometimes.

I looked around his room. It was very neat, since there was hardly anything in it. His bed was unmade, of course. (Bill had promised that James would learn bed-making at WCDI when he got older.) A Tinkertoy structure stood in one corner. It had been there for weeks.

Then I spotted something red behind James's feet.

"Hey, James, what are you up to? What are you hiding?"

"Ha."

"James, come here," I said, just the way Edie always said it.

He stepped forward.

Behind him was my old red superball. How had James gotten it? It had been out in the garage for months.

"You want to play ball!" I exclaimed. "Is that it?" James had never been interested in anything like that. But the ball must have made the thumping sound.

"Oh-*ma*."

"Well, hey, terrific." So the Z's could wait. "Come on, let's get you dressed." I pulled James's jeans and a faded N.Y. Mets T-shirt out of his dresser and helped him into them.

"Hmm-hmm-hmm," he hummed softly. It was the theme from some TV show.

"Mom'll probably make you change later if she wants us to go to church," I told him, trying to make conversation, "but these'll do for now."

"Hmm-hmm-hmm." He switched to classical.

When he was dressed, I tiptoed over to his door. James followed me. And without my saying anything, he slipped his hand into mine. A peaceful moment. It was so un-James-like. I hoped it would last awhile.

We walked quietly downstairs, and I put our jackets on us.

"You bring the ball, James," I said, just to see what he'd

do. And like any regular almost-five-year-old, he ran into the living room where we'd left the ball while we put on our jackets, grabbed it off the couch, ran to me, and tried to open the front door. I was amazed.

"Do you want to go *out?*" I asked him.

"At," he repeated.

"Good boy!" I cried. Then I had an idea. I touched the superball. "James, *ball,*" I said. "Say ball."

"Ba!"

"Good boy!" I touched the front door. "Door. Say door."

"Doe."

I touched my hat. "Hat."

"Hah."

What did my parents know? James was getting better practically in front of our eyes. *See, I told you so,* I'd say when they got up.

I opened the door, letting the morning sun stream in.

James stood in it, looking dazed.

"Come on," I said, closing the inside door behind us and holding the screen door open.

James just stood there.

"Come *on.* Bring the ball. You've got the ball." I gave him a little shove onto the porch and ran past him down the steps. "O.K., toss it to me," I cried, turning to face him.

James wasn't listening. He wasn't even looking at me. He was gazing into that sun.

"Hey, it's Jonno, remember? Throw me the ball."

"Weee-oooh, weee-oooh, weee-oooh," he whispered.

"Aw, *James,*" I said angrily.

He let me lead him onto the lawn, but it was no good. He wouldn't do a thing. He was way off in outer space or somewhere.

What *hap*pened? I wanted to shout at him. What *hap*pened?

And that was the end of Easter, as far as I was concerned. Oh, Lizzie got an Easter basket and I got two new baseballs and about a pound of bubblegum, and James got a special Lego kit, and then I helped Lizzie and James hunt for Easter eggs, and we did go to church, but I was mad at James all day long. What was he trying to pull? I didn't even tell Mom and Dad how he'd almost said *out* and *ball* and *door* and *hat*.

On Wednesday, Lizzie and I visited James at his school. In fact, our whole family went. We got there around eleven o'clock. James had left on his school bus at eight-thirty.

From the outside, WCDI didn't look like much. It was in the middle of downtown Weston, which is a nice enough little town, but the school just didn't look like a school. We drove along Ashton Avenue, the main street, passing by Woolworth's and Kentucky Fried Chicken and Jane Read's Lingerie and a few real estate offices and beauty parlors. Finally Mom parked the car in front of a flower shop. We all piled out.

"This way, kids," Dad said.

We walked a little farther until we came to a glass door sandwiched between Russo's Hobby Shop and the Shoe Tree. The door was very small and simply had a *12* on it.

Inside, a long, dark hallway led to the back of the building, and a flight of stairs led the way to the second floor.

"Upstairs," said Mom.

We followed her.

I glanced back at Lizzie once as if to say, *"This* is a school?"

She shrugged.

But things were different upstairs. Mom opened a door that said *WCDI* on it and had a picture of a huge helping hand reaching out to a very small boy and girl, and suddenly we could hear school sounds—teachers talking and paper rustling and a few little voices and somewhere a piano playing.

We stepped into what was sort of a combination hall and reception area. A long row of cubbies stuffed with jackets lined the left side of the room. Across from them, a friendly looking young man was seated at a desk surrounded by stacks of paper.

"Hi," he said cheerfully to my parents.

"Hi, Tom," said my mother. "Meet Jon and Lizzie. Kids, this is Tom. He's WCDI's secretary. I think the school would be lost without him."

"Lost in a blizzard," grinned Tom, indicating all the paper. Lizzie giggled.

"Well," said Tom, "you're here to see James, and right now he's in..." Tom checked a huge chart hanging on the wall over his desk. "He's in Self-Help Skills. With Andrea. Take a right, go in the fourth door on your left, and be very quiet. You know what to do. Why don't you leave your coats here? I'll hang them up for you."

"Thanks," said Dad.

We gave our coats to Tom and turned down the hall.

"Hey, this place is *big!*" exclaimed Lizzie.

"Shh," said Dad. "School, remember, Lizzie? Yes, it is big. It's the whole top floor of two buildings. There are eight classrooms, an office, and a large room used for lunch and group activities."

"Where do they go for recess?" whispered Lizzie.

"Back down the stairs and through that long hallway. There's a small playground in the middle of the block."

"Oh."

We walked slowly through the hall, peeking in a few doors. The rooms looked pretty much like regular school classrooms except for the kids. There were usually no more than five in each room, and some of them, like James, looked much too little to be in school, while others looked much too big. Bigger than Edweird, even. One class had only two kids—and two teachers!

We reached the fourth door on our right, and Dad said, "When we go inside, we'll be in a small, dim room. We can't turn the lights up because the walls of the room are two-way mirrors, and if the room becomes too bright—"

"What're two-way mirrors?" interrupted Lizzie.

"Oh, sorry, honey," said Dad, "I thought you knew."

Lizzie shook her head, putting on that frustrated look she sometimes gets because of James. She pulled her baseball cap tighter over her ears.

"It's O.K.," said Dad. "A two-way mirror looks like a regular mirror on one side, but from the other side you can see *through* it, like a window. Now, this little room we're going into is between two classrooms. The side wall of each classroom looks like a mirror to the children, but when we're in the little room, we can see right into the classrooms. In other words, we can see the kids, but they can't see us. Get it?"

"Yup," said Lizzie.

I nodded.

"Now, the mirror works best for us if we keep the lights dim, so you'll just have to let your eyes adjust to the darkness. Also, we have to be very quiet, because even though the children can't see us, they can hear us."

We stepped into the room. It was lit with a funny yellow-brown light. There were a lot of chairs in the room, and a woman was seated in one, pulled up to the window, gazing intently into the classroom on the right. She glanced at us when we came in, but then went back to looking.

"Which is James's classroom, Mommy?" whispered Lizzie.

"I'm not sure. Let's see..."

"I see him!" I hissed. "He's over there." I pointed to the class across from where the lady was. We all pulled up chairs to the other window.

"Not too close," cautioned Dad. Lizzie was practically pressed into the glass. She leaned back a little.

James was in a room with three other kids and two teachers. Two of the kids, a boy and a girl, looked just a little older than James. Another boy looked as if he were about my age. They were sitting in a row in small wooden chairs.

And they were all in their underwear. The kids, I mean. Not the teachers. "Mo-om," I yelped when I saw this.

"Shh. Just watch," she whispered.

The teachers, who were also sitting on little wooden chairs, were facing the kids. The kids' clothes were in piles in front of them. "O.K.," one teacher said. "James and Nicole, put your *pants* on."

The little girl leaned forward, found her pants, and started to put them on.

James did nothing.

"James, put your *pants* on." The teacher guided James's hand to his blue jeans.

It was a slow process that took almost five minutes and a lot of prompting, but James did get his pants on. He was rewarded with Cheerios an a gigantic hug.

We watched for half an hour while the four kids worked on getting dressed. James was the slowest, but then he was probably the newest, too. The little girl, Nicole, was pretty good, and the big boy could even button his shirt. It would probably take a long, long time to teach James how to button, I thought.

After Self-Help, we watched James have a speech lesson with Edie. She was trying to teach him his name—both parts—because what would happen if he ever got lost and couldn't even say his name? But James was having a lot of trouble saying his name.

In fact, he spent most of the time fidgeting and jumping out of his chair. Each time he jumped up, Edie patiently sat him back down, saying, "No, James," firmly. The few times he did sit still, Edie made sure he got plenty of hugs and Cheerios. Then she'd start in with the speech lesson again.

"James, what's your name? Say 'James.'"

A couple of times James looked at her, and looked like he might be thinking about repeating his name, but he never did. Instead he'd stand up or squirm or weee-oooh.

I was amazed at how patient Edie was.

When Speech was over, it was lunchtime at WCDI. All the kids and teachers went to the big room and spread out their lunches on two long tables.

Bill called us into his office.

"Nice to see you," he said as we were sitting down.

Lizzie smiled. She really likes Bill. "How's the fund-lifting going?" she asked.

"Fund-raising," corrected Bill gently. "Not too badly, Lizzie. We made about three hundred dollars at the sale on Palmer Square, but we have a long way to go."

Oh, no. I had hoped for better news. James needed all the help he could get. "What's next?" I asked anxiously.

"With the fund-raising?" asked Bill.

"Yeah."

"Actually, Mr. Holtz—he's the chairman of the fund-raising committee—has a clearer idea than I do. But I think a big dinner is coming up."

"A dinner with songs and speeches?" asked Lizzie.

"Exactly like that."

Mom and Dad and Bill began discussing James then. He was making progress, Bill said. Good progress in some areas, slow progress in others.

What's *really* going to happen to him? I wanted to ask. Is he going to be normal? But I didn't say anything. I knew nobody had the answers to those questions.

On Saturday evening we celebrated James's fifth birthday. We had dinner first, and James ate some hamburger and carrots with just about no complaints. Then Lizzie and I cleared the table, and when we were seated again, Mom carried in a big chocolate cake and set it in front of James. It said HAPPY BIRTHDAY, JAMES in yellow frosting and was decorated with candy circus clowns. Five blue candles (plus one to grow on) were stuck in it, but they weren't lit because James isn't always too good with fire, and he wouldn't know how to blow them out, anyway. But we sang to him, and James gazed at the ceiling with a funny half smile. Then Mom served up the cake, and James discovered he liked chocolate. But after a couple of mouthfuls he got wiggly. When he began smearing chocolate in his hair and on the tablecloth, Mom decided dessert was over.

Presents came next. We sat around in the living room. Lizzie had insisted on wrapping all the gifts. "You *have* to. It's a *birth*day," she'd said.

But she got mad when James wouldn't open them. He didn't know what "open" meant or how to tear off the paper or anything. So he sat there with the first present in his lap and diddled the ribbon between his fingers.

"Open it," commanded Lizzie.

James let the present slide to the floor.

In the end we opened all his presents for him. James sat solemnly, sometimes looking on, sometimes humming softly.

At last all the gifts were spread on the floor in front of him. Mom and Dad had gotten him a fancy set of new building materials called Construx, two new shirts, a pair of Snoopy bathing trunks because he was going to have swimming lessons at WCDI this summer, an easy wooden puzzle, and a tricycle. Lizzie had made him a storybook called "Bruno, the Big Bad Bear," and I had gotten him his very own red superball, just in case.

James reached out, and we all leaned forward, eager to see what new toy he wanted first. I watched his hand close over a fistful of shiny blue wrapping paper. With his other hand, he grabbed for some yellow paper. Then, giggling and squealing and calling out "oh-*ma*," he scrambled around the room, crinkling the paper and tearing it and flinging it in the air. His presents sat ignored in the middle of the floor.

Lizzie disappeared. A few minutes later I saw her outside, swinging alone on her monkey swing in the falling darkness.

Happy birthday, James, I thought.

15. Getting Even

The day after James's birthday party was the last day of spring vacation. A good thing, too. Pete and Termite and I were bored practically out of our skulls. A little freedom goes a long way.

I was really glad when Pete called me that morning.

"Hey, Mac," he said. "Want to go to the roller rink? Termite and I are going."

"Yeah!" I said. "That sounds good." I'd delivered my papers and didn't have any plans for the rest of the day. "Would you mind if I asked Lizzie? She might want to get out of the house." I was remembering her after the party last night. "I mean, she wouldn't have to skate with us or anything. She can find her own friends when she gets there." I hoped.

"O.K.," said Pete. I could tell he was shrugging.

"Who's driving?" I asked.

"My mom. Come over at noon."

"O.K. Thanks. See you."

I ran upstairs. "Lizzie!" I yelled. Her darn door was shut again. It couldn't be James. Dad had taken him to the playground while Mom worked on a writing project.

"Lizzie?" I knocked on her door.

"Just a minute," she called. She opened the door a crack and peered out.

"Um, can I come in?"

"We-ell." She eased herself through the door, closing it behind her as she stepped into the hall. "We—we can talk out here."

"What are you doing?" I demanded.

"None of your business, Jonathan Eckhardt Peterson."

"Hey, O.K. Do you want to come to the roller rink with Pete and Termite and me?"

"Today?"

"No, Memorial Day."

"Come *on*."

"Of course today, Lizzie. Around noon. Mrs. Wilson's driving."

"Oh, thanks, but I can't." She started to squeeze herself back into her room.

"Lizzie, what *are* you doing? Why can't you come with us?"

She paused. "I'm busy."

"With what?"

Another pause. "All right, you might as well see now. You're going to find out sooner or later. I was going to start today, anyway."

"Start?"

She opened her door all the way, and I looked into her room. It was the hugest mess I'd ever seen. Junk everywhere. Scraps of felt and pieces of yarn clinging to the rug and the bedspread. The wastebasket overflowing with stuff, spilling out onto the floor.

"Mom is going to kill you," I said flatly.

Lizzie nodded. "That's one reason the door was closed."

"Well, what on earth *is* all this?"

"It's a project. I learned some of it in Brownies, and then my art teacher helped me."

"What *kind* of a project? Come on, Lizzie. Just tell me."

"It's easier to show you," she said. She tiptoed over to her bureau, picking her way through the junk. Then she opened the bottom drawer and removed a layer of neatly folded shirts. "These shirts are camouflage," she said. "When Mom sees a drawer looking so neat, she always leaves it alone." Lizzie laid the shirts on her bed. "Come here, Jonno."

I stumbled to the bureau.

"Look," she said.

I looked. In the drawer were stacks of pretty felt things. "Those are really nice. . . . What are they?"

"This pile here is eyeglass cases." She took one out. "See?" The letter *M* was on it.

"What's that *M* sewn on for?" I asked.

"It's not sewn on; it's embroidered. I can do any letter of the alphabet. These are *monogrammed* eyeglass cases."

I could tell she was proud of the word. "Hey, wow! Good idea, Lizzie. What else have you got?"

"This pile's monogrammed bookmarks, and this pile's monogrammed change purses, and this pile's monogrammed handkerchiefs, only there aren't too many of them yet, because you have to buy plain handkerchiefs first, and they're a little expensive. For me."

"This is pretty terrific, Lizzie. Really."

"Thanks."

"What are you going to do with it all?"

"Sell it. Door to door. I know it didn't work with your seeds, Jonno, but maybe this would be different. People might buy them as gifts or something. Also, I get to keep *all* the money I earn."

"And you're going to start selling today?"

"Yup."

"Wow."

"I better get back to work. I've got to clean all this stuff up before Mom sees."

"Yeah. . . . Hey, Lizzie, how come you kept this such a big secret?"

Lizzie contemplated me from under her red cap. "I was afraid you'd laugh," she said at last.

"Laugh? Why would we laugh? When have we ever laughed?"

"Not really too often, I guess. It's just that you and Pete and Termite always think up such great ideas. I didn't think I could come up with one as good as yours."

"Oh. Well. . . you did."

Lizzie grinned.

"Good luck today," I said, closing her door behind me.

"Thanks!" she called.

"O.K., boys," Mrs. Wilson said as she dropped us in front of the roller rink. "Just give me a call when you're ready to come home."

"Oh, I almost forgot!" I cried. I slammed the car door shut and leaned in the front window toward Pete's mother. "My mom said she'd pick us up this afternoon since you drove us here. So we'll call her, O.K.?"

"Oh, that's fine, Jon. See you later, boys."

We waved and ran through the big double doors to the rink. We headed straight for the skate rental booth, paid our money, and then sat down on the benches by the rink to lace up.

I hadn't gotten further than about two laceholes when Pete elbowed me. "Hey, look over there!"

I looked across the rink in the direction he was pointing,

but didn't see anything. "What?"

"There. It's Edweird. And some woman."

"You're kidding!" I jumped up, forgetting my skates, and my feet almost shot out from under me. I regained my balance and craned my neck around.

Suddenly I spotted them on the other side of the rink, moving slowly along, clinging to each other and hugging the railing at the side. Edweird looked like he was dressed for a roller derby or something. He was in these bright blue-and-gold shorts and a bright blue-and-gold tank top with a *24* on the back. And his fat was showing everywhere.

I sat down, gawking.

"Geez," said Pete, "where does he think he is? The Olympics for the Fat?"

I smiled uneasily.

Edweird and the woman inched their way around the rink. By this time, Pete and Termite and I had pretty much given up on our skates and were just staring.

The woman looked a lot like Edweird. She was heavy, with dark wavy hair and brown eyes. And while she wasn't dressed like Edweird, she didn't look like she belonged in a roller rink. I mean, she still had her coat on, and it wasn't like the rink was freezing cold or something.

"I bet that's Edweird's mother," I hissed.

"Yeah," smirked Pete. "Mrs. Edweird."

I couldn't figure out what they were doing here. Obviously they didn't skate well; they could barely stand up. They didn't look like they were having any fun. Maybe Edweird thought it was the thing to do. The kids from our class came skating here a lot. But why had he come with his mother? Then again, who else would have gone with him?

The three of us watched their progress around the rink with interest. Finally we turned back to our skates. Termite finished lacing his first. He stood up, and just as he did so a bunch of kids whizzed by him and snatched his Mets cap off his head.

"Hey!" he shouted angrily.

I heard familiar laughter. Four figures crashed to a halt at the side of the rink. David, Alan, Hank, and Chris.

"Give it!" yelled Termite, ready to fight.

"O.K., O.K.," Hank came back, even though everyone was supposed to be going around the rink in one direction and he had to skate against the flow. He handed Termite the cap.

"Did you see?" asked David, skating back to us, too.

"Edweird?" I asked.

"Yeah," laughed David. "What a jerk. With his *mother.*"

We all laughed, only my heart wasn't in it for some reason.

Suddenly the in-boys took off. "Watch this!" Chris shouted to us. The four of them charged around the rink, skates flying, doing about eighty miles an hour. They skated right up to Edweird, then darted around him and turned to face him, skating backward while Edweird and his mother crept forward. Edweird's mother looked annoyed. She was saying something to the boys. She shook her finger at Chris.

The boys took off again, doing another turn around the rink, then slowing down as they caught up to Edweird and his mother. This time, they dogged along behind them, talking to them, teasing them. "Who's your girlfriend, Ed*weird?*" I heard Alan jeer as they neared us.

"Boys," Edweird's mother admonished, but she sounded nervous as well as mad. Just then she lost her balance and fell down with a thud. Edweird, startled, gave her his hand and tried to pull her up, but he fell, too. With shouts of laughter, the in-boys left Edweird and his mom struggling on the floor of the rink.

And suddenly I remembered the day not so long ago when Pete and Lizzie and I had taken James to the school playground.

I remembered the horrible feeling, like a kick in the stomach, when I heard the kids laughing at James, teasing him, making fun of him for eating gravel and taking his clothes off and weee-ooohing and flapping his hands. How dared they?

And now I felt the rage all over again, only this time I wasn't angry at a bunch of neighborhood kids for teasing James; I was angry at the in-boys for what they were doing to Edweird. Edweird couldn't help being the way he was any more than James could help being the way *he* was.

Without thinking, I leaped out of my seat and sped around the rink, Pete and Termite right behind me, until I caught up with Chris, and grabbed him by his shirt collar.

Chris's feet shot out from under him, but he clambered for the railing and managed to stay upright. "Hey!" he yelled in surprise. He turned to face me. "What do you think you're doing?"

"Leave Edwei—Edward alone," I panted.

Chris looked at me as if I were crazy.

The rest of the in-boys and Pete and Termite gathered around us, watching uneasily. Edward and his mother, who had managed to get up and start skating again, stopped a few yards away and were watching, looking both interested and confused.

"Leave . . . him . . . alone," I repeated slowly.

"Since when do I take orders from you?" yelled Chris.

Alan, Hank, and David moved closer to us.

Pete and Termite moved closer to them.

Edward's mother, looking like an angry hornet, started to stomp over to us, only she was too unsteady on her skates.

"I'm tired of your being such a big shot," I said to Chris.

"Oh, yeah?" he threatened.

At that point, Mrs. Jackson grabbed Edward by the wrist

and pulled him off the rink. Edward kept stumbling because he was watching me over his shoulder. His eyes were wide and staring, as if he couldn't believe what was happening. I didn't blame him. *I* used to tease him.

Chris inched his face closer to mine.

"Yeah!" I yelled back.

Chris jumped in surprise, then raised his fist to sock me one.

"Run!" hissed David just then. "Here comes the manager."

I turned, and over my left shoulder I could see a big man striding toward us. He was wearing a red blazer with an emblem on the pocket, and was followed by a couple of the guys who worked at the refreshment stand. Mrs. Jackson must have warned them about us. I thanked her silently.

The seven of us scattered, and melted into the crowd before the manager could catch us.

"Let's go," I said raggedly to Pete and Termite when we reached the bench we'd left our jackets on. My breath was coming in gasps, my chest heaving, from fear as much as from the fast skating. With shaking fingers, we unlaced our skates, yanked them off, and left them on the floor.

Ten minutes later we were outside, and my fear was fading away. I'd done it! I'd really done it! I'd stood up to Christopher Giancossi. I'd fought with him—sort of—and I'd said what I felt about Edward. Maybe I'd never be one of the in-boys, but at least I was being honest, and that would mean a lot to the kids I liked best—Pete and Termite, Steph and Claud.

I realized I didn't care one bit what Chris or Hank or Alan or David thought.

16. Pete's Brilliant Idea

"Hey, Mac! Hey, I swear—I swear on a stack of Bibles—I've just had the most brilliant idea in the whole world!"

I turned around, almost falling off my bike.

It was Sunday, a week after the afternoon we'd spent at the roller rink, and it was only six forty-five in the morning. I was just finishing up my paper route, and out of the blue, Pete had appeared, pounding along the sidewalk behind me.

"Pete, geez, what are you doing? You nearly scared me to death. Nobody's up at this hour, except the other paper route kids." I put on the brakes and stopped at the end of our driveway.

Pete dropped down on the grass near me. I parked my bike and flopped next to him.

"Who can sleep?" asked Pete. "It was about six this morning and I woke up with a jolt, thinking this great idea. I don't know where it came from. Maybe a dream or something."

"So what is this great idea?"

"That we give a carnival!" cried Pete. "Wouldn't it be terrific? You and Termite and me. It would really be fun, and we'd probably earn a ton of money. We can have games with prizes and a refreshment stand and a raffle and *every*thing!"

"Yeah..."

"We can make up signs and post them all over the place, maybe even put an ad in the paper, so everyone will know about it. Think—lots of little kids will come, and we'll charge like twenty-five cents or something for each game. We could make a fortune, and the kids will have fun, of course. After it's over, we'll divide all the money three ways. You'll probably have enough to get the automatic baseball pitcher—and maybe more left over—and then we can start planning the training institute for the sum—"

"Wait, Pete. I can't think that far ahead," I complained.

"Well, what about the carnival?"

I chewed on a piece of grass. "I think it's a good idea," I said finally.

"Good. Now, first we have to make lists. Lots of lists."

"Unh-unh."

"Unh-unh?"

"First I have to have breakfast. And I promised Lizzie I'd help her with something this morning. But how about right after lunch?"

Pete looked disappointed.

"You can tell Termite about it this morning."

"O.K.," said Pete. He leaped up and charged across the lawn to Termite's house.

"I'd wait'll they're all up," I yelled after him.

Pete turned and waved, and I headed into my house. There was no one quite like Pete when he was starting up a project, I thought. There was no one quite like Pete, period.

That afternoon, Pete and Termite and I finished our weekend homework in a big hurry and met at Termite's house for a carnival meeting. We chose his house because no parents were around.

"What first?" asked Termite.

We were slumped around the floor in Termite's rec room, drinking Cokes and eating potato chips out of the bag.

"Lists," replied Pete definitely.

"Lists?" asked Termite.

"Yeah. A list of booths we'll have at the carnival, a list of things we have to do, a list of things we have to buy—"

"Like what? I mean, what do we have to buy?" asked Termite.

"Oh, lots of stuff. Oak tag so we can make signs, ad space in the *Tribune,* prizes for the games, junk to sell at the refreshment stand..."

"And where are we going to get all this—this advance money?" I asked skeptically, although I was pleased with myself for coming up with one of those fancy terms Pete always uses.

Pete cleared his throat. I could tell he was going to hedge.

"Be honest," I said firmly.

He cleared his throat again. "We could borrow it."

"From the bank?" I asked, knowing darn well that wasn't what he meant. I crossed my arms and glared at him.

"We're too young to borrow from the bank," put in Termite, looking from Pete to me and back again. "To borrow from the bank you have to be able to put up Uncle Latimer. My dad said."

"Collateral," I corrected him. "But Pete didn't mean borrow from the bank. He meant borrow from me....Didn't you?" I accused him.

"Aw, come on, Mac. You've got more money than you know what to do with. This'll put you right over the top for the pitcher or the Starcruiser or anything. You loan us some bucks for the carnival; then when it's all over, we pay you back first, and divide the rest three ways. You can't lose."

"Yes, I can. What if I put up more money than we earn back?"

Pete paused.

"I'm the only one who's got anything to lose here," I persisted.

"So you risk it. It's like buying a lottery ticket. Only you have a better chance of earning money with the carnival than of winning the jackpot."

"I'll have to think about it," I said. "I'll let you know. And another thing. What about Chris and those guys?"

"What about them?" countered Pete.

"You know." Ever since the incident at the roller skating rink, the in-boys and Pete and I had been at a standoff. I had won something, but I wasn't sure what. They didn't speak to us, and we didn't speak to them. Not a word had been said about what had happened. They just ignored us — and Edward. Pete and I had tried to be nicer to Edward whenever we saw him. For one thing, we never called him Edweird, even behind his back. And we said hi to him at least twice a day. Edward always seemed really glad to see us, but he also seemed scared of the in-boys, especially Chris. He must have been more scared than he was glad, because he steered clear of our class whenever possible, coming in late and eating lunch with other kids from the Resource Room. I guess he felt safer with them.

But about the in-boys — I knew things weren't really settled between us, and the carnival might stir something up. They were going to think it was a really jerky idea, just like Time-Savers. They'd probably start in with the cracks and teasing again.

"Let's talk about this tomorrow," I said at last, as uncertain about Chris as I was about letting go of my money. "Meeting adjourned."

We didn't get to have a carnival meeting the next day, though. We all had baseball practice after school, and then I had to deliver the Monday *Tribune,* and then I had homework. All during everything—school, baseball, paper delivering, and homework—I kept thinking about whether to invest some of my money in the carnival. I just couldn't decide. I sure didn't want to put a whole lot of work into the carnival, and then lose half the money I'd earned getting up at five to deliver papers and battle Superdog. On the other hand, a carnival could be a lot of fun, if the in-boys would let us alone, and Pete was right—it could bring in a lot of money, too.

Finally I made my decision and called another carnival meeting. "I've decided," I announced, "to put up the money and ignore the dumb in-boys. The carnival's going to be fun, and we're not going to let anyone spoil it for us."

"All *right!*" shouted Pete and Termite, and we started making plans.

We decided to hold the carnival at Pete's house. He had the biggest backyard. The posters we'd make up would say:

COME TO A CARNIVAL!
Games! Prizes! Food!
Place: 320 Napanee Road
Date: Saturday, May 27th
Time: 10 A.M. to 4 P.M.
Come one, come all!
Don't miss it!

We planned to collect big cardboard boxes to use as stands for our booths, and to spend fifteen dollars of my money on little toys at the dime store to use for prizes, on lemonade mix and popcorn and other stuff to sell at the refreshment stand, and on an ad that would appear in the *Tribune* the week before the carnival.

We also had a big discussion because Pete had said people were more apt to come spend money at a carnival if the carnival was for a good cause.

"What do you mean?" Termite asked.

"You know, like if we were going to donate the money we earn to the Red Cross or something."

"Oh. Well, we aren't," said Termite simply.

"Yeah..."

There was this huge pause.

"Pete," I snapped, "you're not thinking of *say*ing the money is for a good cause and then keeping it, are you? That's lying."

"Well, no, but what about saying the money is for a good cause, and then donating some of what we earn to the good cause, and keeping the rest for ourselves?"

"That doesn't sound quite right, either," said Termite.

It wasn't, of course. And in the end we decided the carnival would not be called a charity event or a fund-raiser or anything. But all the talk had given me a good idea. I wouldn't know if it would work out until after the carnival, though.

It's funny how fast things can go from good to bad or from happy to sad. After that carnival meeting, I went home feeling excited. I had a million ideas, and everything seemed terrific.

Later, Bill and Edie came over, and James showed off his stuff. He repeated the words *hi* and *'bye,* and looked at Edie once. It wasn't much, but it was an improvement.

A couple of hours later, things went bad. Bill and Edie had left, and James and Lizzie and I were in bed, only I wasn't asleep yet. I was too excited about the carnival. I lay awake for what seemed like a year, and finally got up for a drink of water.

I tiptoed down the dark hallway, listening to Mom and Dad, who were talking in the living room. Something about their voices made me stop and listen, even though I knew it was eavesdropping.

"I still think we should prepare ourselves for it," Dad was saying.

"I agree with you," answered Mom. "I'm just pointing out that it could be several years from now. We can't give up on him."

Give up on who?

"I'm *not* giving up on him," hissed Dad. He sounded as if he wished he were shouting. "But we can't live in a dream world. We'll make ourselves crazy, too."

Crazy, too. They were talking about James. And they were calling him crazy.

"Well, putting him in an institution will make *me* crazy. He's only a little boy."

An *institution*. What was happening?

I couldn't keep it inside. I ran downstairs and stood glaring at Mom and Dad.

"Jonno?" asked Dad tentatively.

"What?" I was trying very hard not to cry, trying so hard my throat was aching.

"What's wrong?" asked Mom. "Are you sick?"

I shook my head. "I heard."

"Oh." She and Dad looked at each other.

"Come here, son."

Mom and Dad made space for me on the couch, and I sat down between them. Dad put his arm around me.

"It's not for right away," said Mom, "and it's still only maybe."

"But I thought all that changed when we got James into WCDI."

"Honey, James has a *chance* now. But he's still a very slow, very handicapped child."

"But he's smart," I protested. I couldn't let this thing go.

"He may be smart, but he can't dress himself—" began Dad.

"Yet," I interrupted.

"—he rarely speaks, he's not toilet-trained, he'll probably never learn to read, he can't take care of himself, and he barely knows who his family is," continued Dad.

"But he's *learn*ing," I said angrily.

"Jonno, I'm not going to argue with you," replied Dad. "I know it sounds cruel, but institutionalizing James is still a possibility. That's all there is to it."

"How about—" I began.

"No 'how abouts.'"

I glanced at Mom, who was rubbing her forehead, looking very tired. "We're giving James a chance in school," she said, staring out the bay window at the streetlights. "We're watching him, we're helping him, we're loving him. He's just not moving along very fast."

"Are you saying—"

"We're not saying anything right now," broke in Dad. "Come on, it's been a long day. Everybody to bed.... And Jonno, I'd appreciate it if you wouldn't mention this to Lizzie."

"O.K.," I said. I trudged up the stairs without saying good night. When I reached James's room, I unlatched his door, flicked on the hall light, and peeked in at him.

He was sleeping curled up in a little ball, his blond hair spread across his pillow.

Silently I latched his door again, turned off the light, and crept back into my own bed.

17. The Carnival

The morning of the carnival was warm and sunny. I was relieved, since we hadn't decided what we'd do if it rained. By seven-thirty, Pete and Termite and I had eaten breakfast and were rushing around Pete's backyard, setting everything up.

First we put up the big card table. That was for Pete. He was in charge of the refreshment stand. Then we set out six cardboard boxes. Those were for the game booths. Termite was in charge of two of them, I was in charge of two of them, and Dad had volunteered to be in charge of two of them, after I'd told him about my secret idea.

On each box, we hung a sign with the name of the game printed on it: RING TOSS, GRAB BAG (that was for little kids), SPIN & WIN (another easy game), TENNIS TOSS (that was a hard one), BALLOON BURST, and PENNY PITCH. Then we put all the equipment we'd need for each game on top of the boxes so we could set them up later.

Around eight-thirty, Lizzie lugged over one of our old card tables. She was setting up a booth to sell her felt things. She'd had pretty good luck selling door to door, but she had some stuff left over, and besides, she said this would give her an opportunity to take special orders. Of course, she got to keep the money she earned—she didn't have to give any to us—

but I thought her booth might bring more people to the carnival. We figured we were doing each other a favor.

Lizzie wasn't the only one who decided to get in on the act. Her friend Wendell had some special equipment for inflating helium balloons, so he was going to walk around selling a big bunch of them at the carnival, and also on the street, where he might attract customers. Pete's mom was going to sell plant cuttings taken from the jungle she called her living room, and Termite's mom was going to sell secondhand stuff since the Armstrongs had cleaned out all their closets recently. We thought the mothers would be good for getting other mothers (and hopefully their kids) to the carnival. (My mom couldn't help out because she had to watch James. I sort of hoped she wouldn't bring him over. You never knew what he'd do.)

By ten o'clock we were all set up and ready to go. Pete was behind the refreshment stand with big pitchers of lemonade and Kool-Aid, bags of popcorn, and some trays of cookies and brownies. He was also selling Goody Bags for the little kids to carry all their food and prizes in. We'd spent about two hours yesterday decorating those Goody Bags with magic markers, drawing clown faces and animals and cars on them.

On one corner of the refreshment stand sat a stack of tickets and a bowl full of slips of paper. That was for the raffle, and Pete was selling the tickets as well as everything else. The prize we were raffling off was a radio Termite had gotten for his birthday from his grandparents. He already had two radios and didn't know what to do with this one, so it was just sitting in a box in his room, all brand-new and unused. It was a really nice radio, too. We looked in Kaler's and saw one just like it for $29.99. So we were selling tickets for $1.00. We thought it was a pretty good deal. In front of the bowl of tickets we had stood up a sign that read:

WIN A RADIO!!!
• VALUED AT $29.99 •
• TICKETS FOR JUST $1.00 •
• INCREDIBLE BARGAIN •
TRY YOUR LUCK!!!

I looked around at all the booths, all the people ready and waiting. Mrs. Wilson and Mrs. Armstrong were standing behind their tables, arms folded, chatting quietly. My dad and Termite were checking out the prize situation and making sure they had enough change. Pete was counting cups and napkins for the ten millionth time, Lizzie was pulling at her hair, looking worried, and Wendell was out on the sidewalk, hawking balloons and announcing the carnival. I was slouched between my two booths, the Balloon Burst and the Penny Pitch, surveying the scene.

Everything seemed to be under control.

So why did my stomach suddenly turn over? It was nerves, and I felt awful. Really pukey.

Then it hit me. The in-boys. What if they showed up? And what if Mom brought James over?

My stomach was really going crazy. Very slowly, I took five deep breaths and concentrated on counting to ten with each one. When I was finished I felt a lot better.

Which was lucky, because just then our first customers arrived. They were Rosa, from my seed-selling disaster, and the three little Jordan kids. Teddy was proudly showing off a big yellow balloon he'd bought from Wendell, which Rosa had tied around his wrist.

He ran up to me. "Hi, Jon!" he called. "Look what I got." He held out his wrist.

"That's neat," I said.

"I have one dollar and fifty cents left," he said carefully.

Teddy and James were the same age. Teddy could count money and James couldn't even say his own name.

"Would you like to play Spin and Win?" I asked him. "It's just twenty-five cents, and you get a prize no matter what."

"Really? Yeah!"

All the Jordan kids ran over to try Termite's Spin & Win.

"Hi, Jon," said a voice at my elbow.

I turned around.

Oh my gosh. It was *Adrienne*. Adrienne with the sense of ...humor. And right behind her were Polly, Andy, Michael, Lissa, and Cindy. Bringing up the rear was Mrs. Divine, the grandmother-person. She was trying to watch the kids, but they all scattered. Adrienne headed for me and the Penny Pitch. She would.

And suddenly everything was very busy. More and more people wandered into Pete's backyard. Wendell must have been doing something awfully good or noisy in the street. At any rate, all I could think of was making change, handing out pennies and darts, blowing up balloons, and keeping little kids from getting frustrated or impatient. When I finally had a chance to look at my watch, it was almost noon. I couldn't believe it.

I looked in the cigar box on the Penny Pitch stand. It was full of money. This was great!

"Jon! Pete!" called two breathless voices.

I looked up and saw Steph and Claud parking their bicycles in the driveway and then running over to us.

"Hey, this is excellent!" Steph cried.

"Yeah," agreed Claud. She trotted back across the yard toward Pete.

I handed five pennies to a little boy in blue overalls, and he began tossing them very seriously.

"Listen," whispered Steph. "We thought we should warn you."

"What?" I asked, my stomach sinking.

"The *boys* are on their way over. We passed Alan, Hank, and David on their bicycles at the Giancossi's, waiting for Chris to come out."

"Oh, *no,*" I groaned.

"Did I win? Did I win?" asked the little boy suddenly.

"You sure did," I said, checking the board he'd tossed the pennies on. "Come choose your prize."

He selected an eraser that looked like a piece of bubble gum, and moved over to the Ring Toss.

"Steph," I said urgently. "Would you do me a big favor?" She nodded. "Sure."

"Would you take over for me here while I go talk to Pete and Termite?"

"O.K."

I showed her what to do, and ran to the refreshment stand. "Pete," I said, "I just wanted to warn you. All the in-boys are on their way over. Steph told me."

"Well, O.K. I'll be on the alert."

I gave Termite the news, too, and he nodded, looking scared.

Then I went back to Steph, who needed another pair of hands. So many kids wanted to play both games now that it was too much for one person.

"Here, Jon. You handle the Balloon Burst, and I'll take the Penny Pitch for a while," she suggested.

"Thanks, Steph," I said, flashing her a grateful smile.

For ten minutes everything went smoothly.

Then, just as I was beginning to relax a little, two boys showed up. Not Chris or Alan or Hank or David, but Edward (with his mother) and James (with my mother).

I could have died.

Edward huffed over to me.

"Hi," he grinned.

"Hi," I said trying to sound friendly. I really *wanted* to be friendly, especially after trying so long to make up with him about the business at the roller skating rink. But why did he have to choose this particular time to show up?

"This is a really good idea," he said, still grinning and looking around at the people and booths.

His mother smiled hopefully at me.

"Thanks, Edward," I said. "Do you want to play a game or something?" I checked the driveway to see if the in-boys had arrived yet.

"Sure," he said.

While he was deciding what to play, I heard a sudden explosion of "Weee-oooh, weee-oooh, weee-oooh, weee-oooh, weee-oooh," and some screaming.

James had had it.

Two minutes in the crowd was too much for him. He was squirming and yelling and flapping his hands while my mother tried to pick him up.

Chris, Hank, David, and Alan, of course, showed up in the middle of this. Smirking, they watched as Mom tried to calm James down. She took him to a quiet corner of the yard and held him, talking quietly to him.

Then the boys sidled up behind me and watched Edward, who had decided to throw darts, and had already hit two balloons.

"I want to play," said Chris, shoving a dirty dollar bill in my face.

"Well, you'll have to wait your turn," I said. Edward had two darts to go.

"Well, you'll have to wait your turn," mimicked Chris. "Did you hear that, Alan? He sounds like a stupid teacher."

"How's it going, son?" my father yelled over to me just then. I think he was watching what was going on.

"Fine. Fine, thanks," I shouted back.

Edward threw his last dart. He'd hit three balloons, which was hard to do, and he chose a pencil sharpener as his prize. He showed it proudly to his mother.

"Idiot," muttered Chris, watching him.

"Come on, let's see you do that," I challenged him as I fastened new balloons on the board.

Chris snorted. "A moron could do better."

"Well, in that case, maybe you'd better not play."

Angrily, Chris snatched the first dart out of my hand and aimed at the big bulletin board that was propped up on a chair with five little balloons pinned to it. He threw the dart as if the target were about a mile away. It smashed into the board, just barely hitting a balloon.

Chris glared triumphantly at me, aimed the next dart, and threw it, but not quite as hard as last time.

The dart landed in a big patch of bulletin board.

Steph, Claud, Alan, Hank, and David, who had also gathered to watch, all laughed nervously.

Chris looked as if he wanted to aim the third dart at me instead of the bulletin board.

"Come on. Any moron can do it," I goaded him.

Famous last words. The dart sailed into the center balloon, bursting it with a small pop. I half expected the boys to clap, but everyone was silent.

Chris took the fourth dart from me wordlessly, but managed to give me a look that could have stopped Superdog in midgrowl.

"Last chance, pro," I told him. "You've got to hit one more balloon to tie Edward."

Chris faced the target and closed one eye, aiming carefully. He pulled his arm back and let the dart go.

He didn't even hit the target. The dart landed in the grass.

"Way to go," I said. "Want to play another round?"

Everyone laughed again, and this time the laughter didn't sound the least bit nervous. Even Edward joined in. Chris looked as if he were about to say something, but he kept quiet. He and the other boys turned to leave—and almost bumped into my mother, holding James, who was quiet now. He was smiling slightly and looked pretty normal.

The boys stared for a few seconds, then headed back to their bikes and rode off.

I felt relieved. And pleased. Very pleased.

I signaled over to Pete and then to Termite that everything was O.K.

Four hours later the carnival was over, and everyone was cleaning up. At four o'clock we had held the drawing for the raffle. Rosa had won the radio! She'd been thrilled, and had talked on and on so fast we couldn't understand a word she was saying.

Lizzie had sold everything she'd set up on her table and had taken special orders for six eyeglass cases and two change purses.

By five-thirty Pete, Termite, and I had the Wilsons' backyard pretty well cleaned up. Then the fun began. We took all our boxes full of money up to Pete's room, dumped them out in one gigantic pile on his floor, and started counting.

I couldn't believe it! Even after we paid me back the fifteen dollars I'd lent us to start the carnival, we had each earned over twenty-five dollars. I had enough for the automatic baseball pitcher, *and* enough for my surprise.

I couldn't wait to tell Mom and Dad and Lizzie.

If only I could tell James.

After all, I was doing this for him.

18. Celebrities

On Monday morning, Mom, Dad, Lizzie, and I piled into our car. We were going to school—James's school. (James had left earlier on his bus, as usual. It was better not to disturb his routine.)

I was feeling pretty excited because I was going to get to carry out my surprise. I was going to present fifteen dollars of my carnival money to WCDI for their fund-raising. If the school had more money, then they could help James better, and if they could help James better, maybe he wouldn't have to go to an institution. Of course, I knew fifteen dollars wasn't a lot compared to the thousands Bill said they needed, but I figured every little bit helped. You put enough fifteens together and eventually they'd add up to a thousand or so.

Also, of course, I hadn't told anybody *why* I was giving fifteen dollars to WCDI. There were two reasons for this. One, when I thought about it, I realized I was donating the money more to help James then to help the other kids in his school. That was sort of selfish. And two, I wasn't supposed to talk about James and the institution anyway. So I kept my mouth shut and let everyone think I was being a wonderful, generous person. And who knows, if they all thought so, maybe I was.

But no matter how wonderful and generous I was being, I was a little surprised when Mom and Dad took Lizzie and me out of school to go to WCDI. I mean, fifteen dollars wasn't *that* big a deal.

But on Saturday night, right before I started reading James his story, Mom had said to me, "Jonno, I just got off the phone with Bill. I told him you had something to present to him, and he suggested we all go to WCDI on Monday."

"After school?" I asked, trying to control James, who was getting squirmy.

"No," replied Mom, "in the morning, while WCDI is in session."

"Oh," was all I said. I should have known then that something was going on. But I was too happy realizing I'd miss a math test on Monday.

Monday morning when Mom woke me up, she spent about five minutes rummaging around in my closet.

"Mom," I croaked. "What are you doing?" I don't always sound too polite early in the morning.

"I'm laying out the clothes I want you to wear."

Laying out my clothes? I swear, she hadn't done that in at least four years. "Why?" I asked.

"Never mind. Just wear them."

"Why?" I asked again. They had to be pretty awful if Mom was being so firm at seven in the morning.

I managed to sit up, and sure enough, she'd laid out my gray suit—and a necktie. Those were the worst clothes I could think of. "Mo-om," I complained, "those—"

"No arguments, Jonno."

"Are you laying out Lizzie's clothes, too?"

"Yes, I am. Now get a move on."

"Does Lizzie get to argue with you?"

"No. And if you don't stop, I'm going to...going to..."

I grinned. Mom can never think up threats.

She grinned back. "Put them on. Breakfast will be ready in twenty minutes."

"O.K."

Those clothes should have been another clue that something was up. But at that hour my mind wasn't operating fast enough to solve any mysteries.

We arrived at WCDI around eleven o'clock. This time Lizzie and I knew where we were going, and trooped right up the stairs to greet Tom.

"Well," he said, "here's Jon, our—"

He broke off as Mom came in behind us. I turned around and saw her shake her head frantically at him.

Before he could say anything else, Bill joined us.

"Hello, everybody! Jonno, Lizzie, don't you two look nice."

This came as a surprise to me, since I felt hot and stuffy and itchy.

"James is having a speech session with Edie. Why don't you go watch?"

So we did for a while, spying from a dimly lit room, watching James struggle over his name. He wasn't saying anything yet, but he looked like he might be concentrating better. He was sitting still longer, and looking at Edie more often.

I smiled and glanced at Dad to see him smiling, too. He couldn't possibly put a five-year-old in an institution...could he?

When James's class was over, Edie led him to the music room and then directed Mom, Dad, Lizzie, and me to Bill's office. I was going to present Bill with the money now, and even though there was no reason for it, I began to feel a little nervous—hotter and stuffier and itchier than I did already. My face was probably the color of a pomegranate.

I patted my pocket where I had tucked the envelope for Bill. A crisp, new ten-dollar bill and a crisp, new five-dollar bill were inside. At first I had had nine ratty one-dollar bills, twelve quarters, nineteen dimes, sixteen nickels, and thirty pennies, but Dad had traded me the ten and the five so I could be neater.

We stepped into Bill's office—and to my surprise, Bill wasn't the only one in it. Two men with pencils stuck behind their ears and pads of paper in their hands, and a woman holding a camera with this huge flash attachment, were crowded in as well.

"Surprise, Jonno!" said my mother. "These are some of your co-workers from the *Tribune*."

For a minute, it didn't register. What did WCDI have to do with my paper route?

I guess I looked pretty confused, because Bill stood up and said, "The *Tribune* wants to do a story on you, Jon. It's not every day someone your age donates his money to a school. You're news!"

"Wow!" I said, ignoring the reference to my age. It was not the moment to be insulted.

Then one of the reporters started asking me all these questions: how old I was, where I lived, where I went to school, how I earned the money, and then a bunch of questions about James and the rest of my family.

Mom and Dad and Lizzie lined up along the back wall of the office, watching me and grinning like crazy. I guess they'd all known about the newspaper story.

I answered the questions as best I could. Then the lady with the camera took some pictures of me, and some pictures of me with Mom and Dad and Lizzie. Finally another teacher brought James into the office. He weee-ooohed nervously (James, of course, not the teacher), but even so, the lady got a few pictures of James and me, James and me and Lizzie, James and Edie, and a few other combinations of people. Finally James went back to his music class.

Then one of the reporters said, "O.K., Jon. Now present Bill with the money and we'll take a shot of the actual ceremony."

What ceremony? I was beginning to feel embarrassed. Was I supposed to make a speech? I thought of all the attention I was getting and decided I better live up to it.

I slipped the envelope out of my pocket and handed it to Bill. The camera started flashing. I was seeing spots before my eyes.

"This money," I said proudly, "is for WCDI so you can help James and all the other kids like him." I realized I really meant it.

I glanced across the room and saw Mom sniffling and wiping her eyes, and Dad smiling, and Lizzie giving me our pinkie signal.

Bill took the envelope and said solemnly, "On behalf of WCDI, thank you very much, Jon."

Flash, flash. Flash.

And it was over. What a morning! I'd been shocked at first, but now that everything had had time to sink in, I was pretty excited. I'd never had my picture in the paper, or even my name, except for when I was born, and once when I was one of fifty-eight kids who volunteered to pick up trash on our school playground and the paper printed all fifty-eight of our names.

The reporters and the photographer left, and Bill and Edie thanked me again for the money. "You two are pretty special," said Bill to Lizzie and me. I could tell Lizzie was flattered that Bill thought she was special, too.

"James can be a pain," she said, "but we...we..."

She trailed off and we all looked at her questioningly. She didn't finish, though.

A few minutes later we left, and as we were getting in the car, Dad popped a surprise on us. I didn't know if I could take many more surprises.

"Let's all go out to lunch," he said.

Out to lunch, instead of back to school?

"Really?" Lizzie and I cried at the same time.

"What about school?" Lizzie asked.

"And what about saving money?" I asked.

"I think the four of us deserve a vacation *and* a treat," said Mom.

"All *right!*" I shouted.

So we drove to Howie's Hamburger Haunt and gorged ourselves. And right in the middle of everything, Lizzie said, "Mom, can I have a friend over after school tomorrow?"

I could tell Mom was so surprised she was about ready to shoot out of her seat, but she just said calmly, "Of course, dear. Who is it?"

"Tammy," answered Lizzie casually, as if that cleared everything up.

"Tammy?" asked Mom.

"Yeah, she's in my Brownie troop....I *told* her about James and she said, 'So what?'"

"Very reasonable of her," smiled Dad.

Lizzie went back to her french fries, and that was the end of that discussion.

My thoughts drifted to the newspaper article. I could hardly wait to see it!

19. James Again

The article appeared the very next day, in the Tuesday afternoon edition of the *Tribune*. Those newspaper guys must have
worked pretty fast, I thought, but then, that's what a newspaper
is all about: getting the news out fast.

On my paper route I proudly delivered all those stories about
me, and then tore home with the last *Tribune* tucked safely in
my bag.

"Mom!" I yelled as I threw my bike in the garage and banged
my way into the house. "Mom!"

"Jonno, what is it?"

I found Mom in the kitchen with James. These days, she
usually stopped her copywriting when James got home, and
then worked with him on the things he was learning in school.
I knew I'd probably just destroyed their work session. James
looked up at me, said, "Oh-*ma,*" and started to get off of his
chair.

"Sorry, Mom," I said breathlessly, "but, look."

I spread the newspaper open to page two, and James escaped
to the living room.

"Right on the second page!" exclaimed Mom.

"Yeah," I said.

There was a big picture of me presenting the envelope to Bill, and under that were three smaller pictures: one of me, one of James and Lizzie and me, and one of Edie holding James. James wasn't looking at the camera in either picture, but he was smiling in one, and all in all he looked pretty good.

To the left of all the photos was a paragraph describing them. It read:

> *Top:* Young Jonathan Peterson presents his donation
> to Dr. William Wyman, director of the Weston Child
> Development Institute. *Bottom, left to right:* Jona-
> than Peterson. Jonathan with his sister, Elizabeth,
> and their brother, James, a student at WCDI. James
> Peterson with Edith Rinehart, his speech therapist.

Under the photos was a fairly long article. It started out by telling about me and the carnival. I had very carefully told the reporters Pete's and Termite's full names, and sure enough, they were in the paper, too! Then the article told about our family, and about James and the problems we'd had with him—trying to find out what was wrong with him, then trying to find a school for him. Finally, the article said, we'd placed James in WCDI. Then there was some stuff about Bill and the teaching methods at WCDI, and the progress James was making. It was a little off the subject of the carnival and the money, but that didn't matter. Much. Besides, Mom said with all the publicity for WCDI, people would probably make donations, and that would be wonderful.

Mom and I read the article through twice. Then Mom turned to me and said, "Oh, Jonno, I'm *so* proud of you! You know that, don't you?"

I nodded.

Mom hugged me, and then held me away from her, looking into my eyes. "Dad and I give so much attention to James, sometimes I worry about you and Lizzie."

"Well," I admitted, "it's not always easy. It really isn't. The kids tease me in school. They call James crazy and retardo, and make me feel like *I'm* weird just because James has problems. And Termite's still scared of him. And sometimes James makes me so frustrated I could kill him, but, well, you know . . ."

"Just like Lizzie yesterday," said Mom thoughtfully.

She looked like she might cry, so I was really glad that Lizzie burst into the kitchen just then. Tammy was right behind her. They were wearing their Brownie outfits. Lizzie even had the beanie on, instead of her baseball cap. She didn't seem to care that her hair looked like a Brillo pad.

"Well, hi," smiled Mom. "Hi, Tammy. Nice to see you again."

"Hi," said Tammy shyly.

"See you, Mom. Tammy and I have stuff to do," shouted Lizzie, and she and her friend took off upstairs.

"I guess they didn't want a snack," said Mom.

"I guess not."

We looked at the article once more, and Mom called Dad to ask him to stop in at Cox's on the way home and buy five extra papers so we could send the article to our relatives. I was just about beaming. My teeth would drop out if I smiled any more.

I walked into school the next day feeling awfully proud. I knew the in-boys would probably think the newspaper article was jerky (I mean, it was about my crazy brother and me), but I really didn't care. Steph and Claud wouldn't think it was jerky, and Pete and Termite were so puffed up with pride they were almost exploding. I decided that if this was where being inside out got us, then inside out was O.K.

Just then Steph and Claud charged into the room. "Hey, you guys, this is fantastic!" they were exclaiming.

Claud shoved a copy of the article on my desk. "I brought this in so everyone could see!"

"I can't believe it!" Steph cried. "I've never been in the paper. I never even knew anyone who had an article written about him—except you. Hey, Pete, Charlie, you're mentioned in it, too. Did you know?"

Pete and Termite nodded, grinning.

The next thing that happened shocked me practically out of my shoes. Janie and Elise came into the room, followed by Margaret and Louise. They marched right over to us. Elise had a copy of the article, too.

"Oh, Jon," she exclaimed in this high, false voice. "I think this is just wonderful!"

I glanced at Claud, who rolled her eyes.

"Do you want to sit with us at lunch today?" Elise asked.

"Well," I said, blushing right to the tips of my ears, "um...why don't you eat lunch with Pete and Charlie and Steph and Claud and me?"

Before she could answer, a couple of other kids came over to our group, and then a few more, Edward among them. They all wanted to talk to us. Some of them hadn't read the article yet, but Claud passed her copy around.

Everybody was saying things like, "Neat," and "Great," and "Good idea." I even heard Janie look at the pictures of James and say, "He doesn't look crazy. Are you sure he's the weird one?"

"Well, if it isn't young Jonathan Peterson," said a sarcastic voice all of a sudden.

I looked away from a conversation with Steph and Louise to see that Chris had come in, surrounded, of course, by Hank, David, and Alan.

I decided to ignore him.

So did everybody else, except for Elise who said, "Oh, shut up."

Chris, surprised, did shut up. He looked at a copy of the article, and then at me. Finally, with a sidelong glance at Elise, he said "Nice going, Jon."

"Thanks," I said. I wondered if he might say something nice to Edward then since he seemed to be trying to make up, but he didn't, of course. I guess that was asking too much. Why had I ever wanted to be like the in-boys?

That night at dinner, Mom said, "Edie's coming over tonight for a few minutes."

"Why?" asked Lizzie. "She and Bill were just here."

"I know. I think she has something to show us."

"Hi!" called James from across the table. He wasn't talking to anyone in particular. He was just making noise, but it was a nice change from "weee-oooh."

Lizzie giggled.

I saw Mom and Dad hide smiles.

Edie arrived when I was in the middle of reading to James. When James saw her, he wiggled out of my lap and ran over to give her a hug around her legs.

"Hey, tough stuff," she greeted him.

James leaned back to look at her, giggled, and said, "Oh-ma."

When Mom, Dad, Edie, Lizzie, James, a bowl of Cheerios, and I had all gathered in the living room, Edie said, "O.K., everybody hang on to your hats."

We looked at each other curiously.

Edie sat on the floor facing James, the Cheerios beside her. She made sure she had his attention. When he was sitting quietly and looking at her, Edie said slowly and clearly, "What's your name? Say 'James.'"

James hesitated. "Ja—" he managed to say. "Ja..." He flapped his hands nervously and stood up.

"That's about as far as he gets," said Edie, "but it's a fantastic beginning."

"Hey, I think he just gave himself a nickname!" exclaimed Lizzie. "Jay-Jay! He's Jay-Jay. Now he doesn't have to be James all the time."

Edie was showing us some other things when the phone rang. I ran to answer it.

"Hi, Mac," said Pete's voice.

"Hi. What's up?"

"I've got this amazing idea!" Pete was so excited the receiver was practically jumping out of my hand. "It's for a fund-raiser. For James's school. See, we..."

And Pete was off again. I sat there and listened to his idea and thought about Jay-Jay and WCDI and the carnival. "Don't forget," I said when he stopped for a breath. "This weekend I'm going to go to Kaler's to buy the baseball pitcher. Then we can plan the training institute."

"Right," said Pete.

I heard voices in the front hall then and knew Edie was leaving.

"Pete, I gotta go. I'll see you in school tomorrow. O.K.?" I hung up the phone and ran out in time to yell good-bye to Edie.

Mom and Dad took off for the den to watch TV, and Lizzie decided to call Tammy.

I led James into the living room, thinking it would be hard to start calling him Jay-Jay after all these years. He pulled me over to a Lego building, and tugged on my hand to make me sit down. Then he sat down, too, and began building. He was humming the theme song from *The Flintstones*.

"Do you want help, Jay-Jay?" I asked.

He hummed some more.

I picked up a few Legos and started to put them on the building. James stopped humming and watched me. Then he smiled and went back to work.

About the Author

ANN M. MARTIN grew up in Princeton, New Jersey, and is a graduate of Smith College. Her Apple paperbacks are *Yours Turly, Shirley; Ten Kids, No Pets; With You and Without You; Me and Katie (the Pest); Stage Fright; Inside Out; Bummer Summer;* and the books in THE BABY-SITTERS CLUB series and the BABY-SITTERS LITTLE SISTER series.

Ms. Martin lives in New York City with her cat, Mouse. She likes ice cream and *I Love Lucy;* and she hates to cook.

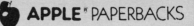